# Wicked
# TEMPTATIONS

## Annie Jocoby

VINCI
BOOKS

# By Annie Jocoby

## Temptations

Vinci Books

vinci-books.com

Published by Vinci Books Ltd in 2026

1

Copyright © Annie Jocoby 2016

The publisher and the author have made every effort to obtain permissions
for any third party material used in this book and to comply with copyright
law. Any queries in this respect should be brought to the attention of the
publisher and any omissions will be corrected in future editions.

A CIP catalogue record for this book is available from the British Library.

Paperback ISBN: 9781036703141

The EU GPSR authorised representative is Logos Europe, 9 rue Nicolas
Poussion, 17000 La Rochelle, France contact@logoseurope.eu

# Chapter One

## Serena

Slade was due to come and talk to me, and I had to admit, I was nervous. Very nervous. He had hinted that he was going to have to do something drastic to make sure that I was safe, and I had a sneaking suspicion on exactly what that thing was going to be. No matter how many times I told him not to do anything that would jeopardize my relationship with him, I knew that he was going to go ahead with his plans. It wasn't going to be pretty.

As I saw him come up the driveway to my house, his head was hung, and I just knew. He didn't even have to tell me what was going on. It was written all over his gorgeous face.

I opened the door, and, without a word, I walked into the sun room. I patted my legs, and the dogs got up on the easy chair with me. Slade, also wordless, followed me into the room and sat across from me. He drew a breath and clenched his hands in front of him. He simply stared at me for the longest time, his beautiful eyes pained and haunted.

I stared back, not saying a single word. In my mind, I was thinking that, if neither of us spoke, maybe none of this would be true. There wouldn't be some kind of awful revelation that hung in the air, threatening to end us. I wouldn't be hearing from him about how he has no choice to marry that bitch, and how he was going to find a way out of it for both of us. How it would only be temporary, and that, soon enough, he and I would be together and there would no longer be a threat to my life. None of that would be true, if only neither of us spoke.

So, for what seemed like an eternity, I sat there, the dogs on my lap, and stared wordlessly at him and he did the same. His hands were still clenched in front of him, and, from time to time, he would hang his head and put his hands behind his neck. Then, a few minutes later, he would look up at me again with pain in his eyes.

Finally, he opened his mouth, as if to speak. At that point, I stood up.

"Don't say it, just don't say it. I already know what's going on. I already know what you told that bitch. And there's only one thing that I can say to you – get the fuck out of my house. Get the fuck out and never, ever come back."

He stood up as well, and attempted to put his arms around me. I pushed him away, violently. "Perhaps you didn't hear me. I want you to leave, and I want you to leave this very second. There is nothing that you can say to me that will make this right." I was being irrational, and a part of me knew it. A part of me, deep down in my soul, knew that what Slade was doing was not only the right thing, it was the only thing that could keep me alive. A part of me knew that what he was doing was sacrificing his own happiness so that I could be safe. That part of me loved him desperately.

The other part of me also loved him desperately, but hated him just as much. That part of me only wanted him and I to be together, no matter how that could be accomplished. That part of me literally didn't care if I lived or died, as long as I could be with him for the short time that I would be on this earth. And he couldn't see that. I hated that he couldn't see that.

These two distinct sides of me were at war as I looked at his beautiful eyes and face. He made no effort to leave, and that made me love, and hate, him all the more. "Serena," he finally said. "I know that you know what happened between Charlotte and me. I know that you know in your heart that I would never do anything like this unless it was absolutely necessary. I think that you also know that I'm going to be get a plan together that will make sure that you and I end up together for the rest of our lives without having a shadow hanging over us. I don't really know exactly what that plan is, but I'm buying time for us. I don't expect you to understand right now, but I would love it if you would please see this as buying our long-term future in exchange for some short-term misery."

I drew a breath. "When is the wedding?" I asked him. I didn't really want to know the answer to that question, of course. I only wanted him to know that I knew what was going on. I wanted to stick the knife into him and make him feel the pain that I felt. By forcing him to answer that simple question, I knew that he was going to feel what he was about to do. To him, to us, to our future. I wasn't buying the whole *I'm doing this now to make sure our future is secure* bullshit.

He could kiss my ass if he thought that I was buying that crap.

He sat back down and hung his head again, putting his hands behind his neck. "I don't know," he said quietly. "Soon. I need to get this over with so that I can start snooping around her family. I need to find a weak spot. I need to find a rat, somebody who is willing to double-cross her and perhaps, maybe, keep her in line." His eyes looked at me, sorrow filling them. "It's the only thing that I can think of right now."

I nodded my head. "Get out. Get out, and go marry your whore. Go marry her, and make sure that your face is in the tabloids at all times." I smiled. "And, trust me, you will be in the tabloids at all times. It's so fucking priceless, this story – rising Hollywood star marries handsome billion-aire who was in the news for a murder he didn't commit. Who is currently about to stand trial for disposing a body and covering up a murder 20 years ago. The tabs are going to be all over that shit."

He crinkled up his brows. "Is that all that you're worried about? That you're going to be forced to see me every time you go to the grocery store?" He made a move, once again, to hold me in his arms, as he stood up and came over to me.

I backed away. With every step he took towards me, I took one step back. He wasn't going to act like nothing was wrong. He wasn't going to be able to just put his strong arms around me, and kiss me and make love to me, as if he wasn't going to be married to somebody else. I wouldn't let him do that. He couldn't get away with that, because I wasn't going to allow that. "Get away, Slade. I told you a few minutes ago that I wanted you gone, and I mean that. Stop the bullshit. You're going to marry that whore, and nothing will be done to save me or to save us. You're going to fall into that lifestyle, and you're going to forget that I exist. I already see that. So get out. Get out now."

"Serena," he began, as he once again wrapped his arms around me.

"No. You and I are done." I pushed him, hard, so hard that he fell on the floor. He apparently wasn't bracing himself. I closed my eyes, and left the room, with him still on the floor.

It didn't take him long, though, to get up off the floor and follow me into the living room.

"Slade, why are you still here? Get out. I told you to get out, and I mean it." I didn't mean it, of course. I desperately wanted him to stay there with me. I desperately *needed* him to stay there with me. But not like this. Not when I knew, *I knew*, that, the second he left the house, he would be leaving for good. He would leave this house and go to her, and, the next thing I would hear, would be news of his happy wedding with the Hollywood goddess. I wouldn't be able to turn on the television without seeing the two of them together. I had always loved to watch the Academy Awards on TV – that was one of my guilty pleasures, even if I hardly ever got to see the nominated movies – but I could never again watch that show, because *she* would be on there with *him*. I would want to vomit when I saw her smiling face, and he would also be smiling, because she would be telling him, behind the scenes, that he better smile *or else*.

Worse than that, though, would be the fact that Slade would no longer be in my life. My life was going to be as empty as it was before I met him, and I just couldn't handle that fact.

"Serena," he said. "I'm not going to even try to bullshit you. I respect and love you too much to do that. So, yes, after I leave, I'll be going to Charlotte's and I'm going to do the unspeakable. I know that there's nothing that I can say to you that will make you believe that this is best for us. I know that you'll never really believe that I'm going to find a way out of this and I'm going to return to you and make you my wife for real. You're going to hate me, and I don't blame you for hating me. I just have to get through these next few months, which are going to be absolute torture, so that I can fix this problem for good. You don't believe that though, and I don't blame you. But I love you, Serena, and, mark my words, we will be together after this. Together for real."

I drew a breath when he said the words *I'm going to make you my wife for real.* That was the first time that Slade had ever said something like that. I had always assumed that Slade wasn't serious about me and my long-term future with him, but, with those words, I knew that he was. That thought comforted me, even though the reality of the situation was that Slade and I, in all likelihood, would never see each other again after today.

I blinked back tears. This was such an impossible situation. The part of me that was desperately in love with him resurfaced for a moment, and I allowed him to come and put his arms around me. I felt his breath inhaling my scent, as if he never wanted to forget it. His masterful hands were gliding up and down the small of my back, and, as I laid my head on his chest, I heard his heart start to pound. I closed my eyes, wanting to stay there forever. If I was ever given a choice just to stand there with Slade, motionless, his arms around me, his heart pounding in my ears, forever, I would have taken it. Forget work, forget Charlotte, forget the world around us. I wanted just to stay there, exactly as we were, for the rest of time.

After what seemed like forever, Slade gently brought my face to his, and kissed me. His hands were on my cheeks, and I felt myself melt into him. Even though my mind was telling me not to do this – it was wrong, he was going to be gone soon, and making love with him would simply make me miss him that much more – my body was betraying me. I felt the heat in his kiss, and I could feel the urgency in it. Both of us knew the score. At least our minds did. But I knew that his body, and his soul, were feeling the need for the two of us to connect one last time. I was feeling the same.

I felt like I had no bones, and Slade picked me up and carried me to my bedroom. He laid me down on the bed, and, without a single word, he gently stripped me of my clothes. When his tongue met my clit, it wasn't with the urgency that he displayed in his earlier kiss, but, rather, it was slow and gentle. It was as if he had to make this last, and he knew it. Every stroke of his tongue brought me to new heights, because I had never felt so much connected to him. I had never before felt like this. It was as if he and I literally were one body, one mind, one heart, one soul. He became a part of me in that moment, and, when I orgasmed for that first time, it was as if it was my very first orgasm ever.

His hands and fingers made their way up my stomach and to my breasts, and his gentle tongue traced a trail up my breasts and to my neck. There was heat in his lips and tongue, heat that I never really felt before. His warmth was something that I had always noted about him, but it was something that I could feel at that moment, more than I had ever felt it in my life.

As I felt his rock-hard cock gently fill me up, I rocked into him, throwing my legs around his back.. I felt as if I never wanted to let him go. I wanted to imagine that I was holding him to me, and that I would hold him to me for the rest of both of our lives. In my head, that was exactly what was going to happen with us – I would keep him there with me, and he would never, ever leave.

He made love to me for the better part of an hour – so slow and gentle that it was almost agonizing. My clit was on fire with every gentle stroke of his glorious penis, which slowly but surely rocked in and out of me. I felt one orgasm after another roil through me. Our bodies were one. I couldn't tell where he ended and I began, or where I ended and he began.

When he finally, and reluctantly, withdrew from me, after I felt his hot cum roiling inside of me, he just looked at me. I looked back at him, and I nodded. There was nothing to say that hadn't already been said. Nothing to do that hadn't already been done.

It was finished. We both knew it. Whether it was finished forever, or just finished for a few months, was unknown. That remained to be seen.

In my mind, though, it was finished for good. I had to just forget about him. If I let myself pine away after him, then I could never move on with my life. And I had to do just that – move on with my life. From that point on, I would pretend like Slade didn't exist. I would just have to compartmentalize him like I always was able to before whenever tragedy struck me.

And that was what this was – a tragedy. Losing Slade was a tragedy.

Just like I moved past all my other tragedies, I would move past this one as well. In time.

At least I hoped that I would.

## Chapter Two

### Slade

I left Serena, and I felt the weight of what had happened come down on me. Goddamn Charlotte. Goddamn her. She was ruining my life, and I knew that I was going to have to find a way out and soon. Very soon. If I had to kill her myself, I would do that. Of course, I didn't want to do that, but that was an option to me right at that moment. I had to admit, covering up that murder for my mother all those years ago gave me a certain kind of confidence that I could do it again. After all, that murder would have been unsolved if it weren't for Charlotte and her big, blackmailing mouth.

As I drove up the highway, my mind was filled with revenge. Revenge was the first thing on my mind, but somewhere, in the recesses of my brain, a plan was starting to formulate. It was hazy though, nascent. At some point, it was going to be fully formed, though, I knew. And then it was going to be put into action.

At that moment, though, I was going to have to face up to what I had done and what was about to happen. As much as it made me want to vomit, I had to face it. I was desperately worried about Serena, too, though – after all, she was still facing danger with Derek. I was going to definitely have to make a deal with Charlotte about that. I was going to have to negotiate with her before we ever got down that aisle, and having Derek either back the fuck off, or, even better, lose his job, would be a part of this negotiation.

---

I finally made it to Charlotte's house, and my mind filled with dread. I looked down at my hands, and they were shaking. I swallowed hard as I drove up the long drive that led to her mansion. As I sat in front of her house, I took a deep breath. I had to feel calm, because my mind had to be clear. Only with a clear head could I figure a way out of this mess.

As I sat in the car, though, Charlotte came bounding out of the house. She came right up to my car. "Did you tell her?"

"Of course."

She looked at me suspiciously. "How did she take it? And was talking all you did?" She backed off the car a few feet and crossed her arms in front of her. She raised an eyebrow as I just stared at her.

*You know that talking is not all we did, bitch.* "What do you think?"

She shook her head. "You don't need to tell me, but I can tell you one thing. That won't happen again. Not with you and her. With you and me, that should happen every single day." Then she smiled. "And, believe me, I will be looking forward to that."

I just stared at her, my hands gripping the wheel. My mind was telling me to run. Run far, run fast, and don't look back. Just go right back to Serena's and whisk her off to my house in Italy, and never, ever, think about Charlotte again.

Of course, we would always be looking over our shoulders. Every minute of every day, we would looking around, wondering when the goons were going to come out and gun us both down.

I couldn't live like that. I couldn't make Serena live like that. So, for now, I had to stay there in that driveway. Staring at that bitch's face. There was nothing else to do, and it made me sick.

Finally, I got out of the car. "Okay, let's go in the house. Let's get our terms straight." I had no leverage at that moment. I knew that. She knew it, too. She held all the cards, because she was the dangerous one of the two of us. She was the one who had the mob ties. She was the one who was desperate and was willing to do anything, absolutely anything, to ensure she got what she wanted.

Still, I was going to negotiate with her as if *I* held all the cards and she had nothing. That was the only way to go into this. If I went into it as if I knew the weak position I had, then she would roll over me. That was the last thing that I wanted, because, well, I wanted to at least ensure that Serena was away from that Derek asshole.

"Come on in," she said, walking into the house. "And let's sit down and try to get this thing done."

I followed her to her terrace, which was set up with a table and chairs and candles as the centerpiece. It looked as if she were anticipating a romantic dinner for two, which is probably what was on her mind. But I was careful to show her, with my body language, that I wasn't having it. None of it. This was a business transaction, nothing more.

I was also going to have to try to negotiate one more term. One major term – that this marriage was going to be a sham in every sense of the word. I would appear on her arm in public. I would do the dance like a marionette. But I wasn't going to touch her in private. There would be no kissing, no dancing, no sex. We would have separate bedrooms.

That was important. Anything else would be truly betraying my love for Serena, and I wasn't willing to do that. Besides, I doubted that I could get it up for her. I hated her that much.

She was certainly trying, though. I glanced at her as she sat across from me, and I noticed that she was wearing something that was plunging. It was a filmy black number that showed her ample cleavage, and she leaned down so that I could see all of her breasts if I was so inclined. I wasn't, of course, so I immediately averted my eyes.

She continued to lean over the table, though. She was attempting to make it impossible to look down her dress. I was just as determined that I wasn't going to.

"Okay," I said, as she poured both of a glass of wine and snapped her fingers. A waiter came around and laid dinner in front of us. We each appeared to have some kind of a stuffed bird, with some asparagus tips with hollandaise sauce and a side of potato. I shook my head. Charlotte obviously had something in mind, and she was going to try her mightiest to get it. "We need to go over terms."

"Go over terms?" she said, apparently incredulous. "You make this all sound like some sort of business transaction."

"Isn't it?"

"No."

"Well, I think that it is. I need to get this straight with you. This is not about love. It's not even about like. It's about Serena's preservation. And mine, to a lesser extent, but mainly Serena's. Don't ever think differently. The second you start to think that what you and I have is real is the second that I get the hell out of here."

She finally stopped leaning over the table, and leaned back in her chair instead. She was sizing me up, trying to find my weak spot, trying to see if I was bluffing her. "What did you have in mind?" she asked me coolly.

"I would like to dictate the terms of this arrangement. First, there will be no physical contact between us. I will have my bedroom and you will have yours, hopefully in two different wings of the house. Second, you will allow me to fire Derek. After all, I am the managing partner of that firm, so I do have the power to fire him. And, considering what he has done to Serena, I do have cause."

She shook her head. "This isn't what I signed up for. Perhaps I should just put that hit back on Serena and be done. Because you aren't giving me a damned thing here."

"I'm giving you the attention that you crave. Being with me will give you just the right air of danger and intrigue to put you in the spotlight. After all, I'm this notorious billionaire who was accused of murder, and most of the people in this country still think that I might have done it. Once we go public, you'll have the cache that you want. Since I know that you want to become this starlet that is in the public eye at all times, then you'll have that with me." I raised an eyebrow. "Take it or leave it."

"I'm leaving it," she said, perhaps too quickly. "I get what you're saying, and you're absolutely right about that – since you were, by far, the biggest story of this past year, and you continue to draw your share of attention, you definitely will be an asset. But I want more than that. I want you and I to be a real couple. That means a shared bed, and that means sex. You can go ahead and fire Derek. I'm through with him, anyhow. But the other stuff is non-negotiable."

I gave her a high opening offer, and I knew that. I also knew that I had to tread carefully with her. "Okay. Thank you for allowing me to fire Derek. We can sleep in the same bedroom, but not the same bed, and there will be no sex between us. Nothing physical between us."

"Why? You're going to be married to me, so you can just forget about that other woman. You might think that you're betraying her by being with me, but you need to stop thinking that. I'm your future. You and I are the ones who will be together. The sooner you understand that, the better off you'll be."

I narrowed my eyes, trying to figure out how far I could push this. If I threatened to walk away, would she acquiesce, or would she get it in her crazy head that she was going to go nuclear? I realized that I wasn't playing with a woman that had a full deck, and that made her inherently dangerous. Yet I couldn't possibly give her what she wanted on this. There was no way in hell that I was going to have sex with her. No way in hell that I was going to touch her in any kind of a romantic way. That was simply non-negotiable.

"Those are my terms. You can take them or leave them." That was the same thing that I said before, and I meant it. Of course, inside, I was a mound of jelly. All she had to do was tell me that she wasn't going to play my game, and that she would just go ahead and put a hit on Serena, and I would have done anything that she wanted me to do.

She sighed. "We'll sleep in the same bed. We don't have to have sex, though. That's my final offer."

I could live with that. As much as I didn't want to, I could. The bed was quite large, as it was twice the size of a king. She usually had her animals sleeping with her, which was why she needed a bed that big. I could certainly have my side of the bed, and she would have hers. I didn't want to think about the possibility that she was going to try to crawl on top of me during the night, though I knew that could happen.

"Okay," I said. Then I dug into the food.

She smiled. "Oh, I love having you dancing on a string like this. Kind of like how you had me doing the same all those years ago. All that time, I was pining away for you. Just pining away. You couldn't give shit less about me, of course, which depressed the hell out of me. Now, here you are, dancing. I love it. I have always thought that turnabout is fair play, but I never thought that it would be quite this delicious."

"It's not going to be as delicious as you have in your mind."

"Oh, but it is. We're finally going to be sharing a roof. I'll finally be sharing your name. I'm going to have you on my arm wherever I go. The paparazzi will never leave us alone." She rubbed her hands together and raised her arms above her head. "It'll be glorious. There's no way the media is going to forget about me. I can just see my Oscar right now." She pointed to a shelf that was just inside the door. "That's where it will be. My agent has already told me that this part I have in this Van Sant film is the part that all the actresses have wanted. It's the part that will make me a star. The only thing that I needed was the right guy to put me into the stratosphere, and now I have him."

It was then that I realized that I might have actually underplayed my hand. I didn't know how desperately she wanted me to give her the kind of exposure that she needed to get her onto the A+ list. She was already on the A list, but, as she had explained to me, there was a tier that was at the very top. It was occupied by the stars who were truly "It" at the moment. The stars whose every move was followed by a stream of paparazzi. She wasn't quite at that, but she would be when she was with me.

I mentally kicked myself. I should have dictated my terms more sharply. I now knew that she would have gone along with anything at that point, as long as she could show up at places around town and have people take her picture. I discounted that too much. I assumed that she was just desperate to be with me, but perhaps she was more desperate for her image to be enhanced.

I had to smile inwardly as I thought about how being with me would increase her cache. I was under investigation for disposing of a body and covering up a murder. I was just out of an investigation for actual murder. I knew that there were many in this country who still believed that I killed poor Jordan Harris. All of this, and she somehow believed that I would be good for her image?

I wondered if there was something in that. Now that I knew that she was more concerned about her image than being with me, I could possibly use that. How I would use that, I didn't really know. But there might be something to that.

The name "Sarah Fuller" popped into my head. The blonde publicist who was slight and tended to drink too much, and spilled the beans when she drank, was the person who might be the one that I needed to talk to. I wondered if she was really going back to Atlanta and become a personal trainer. She might be the person whose brain I could really pick to find out the best way to exploit Charlotte's many weaknesses.

Then again, Charlotte was willing to let her craziness

get out in the press, as well as the murder she committed. That made me despair just a little. If it wasn't for the fact that I strongly suspected that Charlotte was behind my mother's death, I might have been willing to call her bluff a little longer. But, with my mother's death, and the evidence of poison in her system when she died, I knew that Charlotte was a loose cannon. I wasn't quite sure what Sarah Fuller could do to help me if Charlotte was willing to let her cray go public.

As I sat across from her, my mind was whirling a hundred miles a minute. It seemed that my thoughts were careening from one extreme to the next. At one extreme, I was tempted to bolt. I would test her, see if she was willing to make a move, knowing that I was capable of bringing her down in the press. Yes, she claimed that she had all those records erased, but I knew better. Those records were on my system, still, and, while I knew that authenticating them might be a problem, considering that Doctor met his unfortunate end at Charlotte's hands, there was still a chance that the press would be willing to put this stuff out.

But, on the other extreme, I knew that, if there was even a 1% chance of Charlotte making a move against Serena, I had to stay put. I had to be 150% sure that Serena was completely safe before I extricated myself out of this Charlotte mess.

"Okay," I finally said. Charlotte and I had been sitting there, with the food in front of us, untouched, for what seemed like hours. In reality, it had only been a few minutes, but every moment with this woman seemed like hours to me anymore. "So, then, we have an agreement. I appear with you in public, and I guess we share a bed. But no physical touching, let alone sex. I hope that I make this perfectly clear."

She shrugged. I could tell that she was really thinking that she could bide her time with me. She thought wrong, of course. I was going to be firm, absolutely firm, that there would be nothing physical with this woman.

"What's up with that shrug?"

"I think that you're going to change your mind. I can be very persuasive, after all."

"Think what you want."

She sighed. "Well, okay. Listen, tomorrow is going to our first outing together. I've already called the paparazzi to come and follow me." She put her hand to her hair and pursed her lips. She leaned down again, and I steadfastly refused to take her bait. "I'm going to deny, of course, that you and I are together. That just makes the paparazzi more intrigued. That's how the game is played you know. Whip them up into a frenzy before I confirm for them that you and I are getting married. By the time I make this announcement, through my publicist, the media will be going crazy."

"Sounds like you have this all planned out."

"I do. Listen, I've been playing this game for years now. Do you really think that all those actresses or actors who are in the tabloids are in the tabloids because the paparazzi happens upon them or that they had actually called the pap themselves? Nine times out of ten, the pap are contacted and told where to go to get a picture."

I rolled my eyes. I did know that the game is played that way, to be honest. I didn't necessarily think that Charlotte was going to lay it out in such stark of terms, though. "So, what is our first outing?"

"We're just going to go to the beach. I'm going to be wearing a tiny bikini, and, well, we're going to be holding hands and kissing in the ocean."

"I told you, nothing physical." She was already going back on our agreement. That irritated me, and I felt emboldened by my earlier realization about the fact that she wanted me to be her lap dog more than anything.

"Nothing physical behind closed doors. That was my understanding. I told you, though, that I need the pap to think that we're a real couple. That would mean PDA. It's required."

At that, I got up from the table. She wasn't going to push me around like that. While there was a part of me that was apprehensive about calling her bluff, I knew that I had to. There was no way that I was going to act as if I had a weak hand.

"Okay, okay," she said, batting her eyelashes. "We'll hold hands and that will be it. There doesn't have to be kissing and all of that." Then she raised an eyebrow. "You better take this offer, Slade. I'm warning you. I'm at the end of my rope with you, and I know that you don't want your precious whore Serena to have an unfortunate accident." At that, she looked at her nails and then looked back at me.

I sat back down. Holding hands with her wouldn't be all that bad. I sighed, though. Serena was going to be so depressed when she saw me and this spider in the papers. I was going to have to get ahold of her to tell her not to worry. I was only giving Charlotte a little something to keep her in line. I needed Serena to know that.

I crossed my arms in front of me. Charlotte daintily started to eat her food, but I wasn't hungry anymore. "I'll hold your fucking hand." I got up from the table. "I'm going to go and get something eat someplace else. The very sight of your face is making me nauseated."

She smiled and shrugged her shoulders. "I'll see you later."

I knew that she felt that she was winning, and that thought made me not just sick, but it made me want to kill her with my bare hands.

And, if I thought that I could get away with it, I probably would.

# Chapter Three

## Serena

The day after Slade left, I got back to work. I had to. I had no excuse not to. I mean, I could call into work with the excuse that I didn't feel up to working, but that would be just silly. I had been through heartbreak before, and I always showed up to work anyhow. Today would be no different.

Or would it? Yes, I had been through heartbreak before – when my mom died, when I was raped. But nothing quite tore out my soul like what had happened with Slade. I didn't even know why I was so profoundly affected. I only knew that I was.

I got to the elevator, and my heart started to pound. Would Derek be there waiting for me? What about the people in the office – would they know what had happened in my own office? I had intended never to come back, yet, here I was, coming back. I was never one to run away from a problem, even an enormous problem like Derek, and I wasn't about to start now.

Still…I felt my heart pounding so hard, with every floor, that I felt that I was going to pass out. If Derek were there, I didn't quite know how I was going to react. I could tell Harry what was happening. After all, Charlotte was apparently neutralized for the time being. There shouldn't be any danger in telling Harry what was going on.

I finally got to the suite and went in. Peggy, the receptionist, gave me a huge smile. "Serena, it's so good to see you. I have to admit, I was pretty worried about you before. You left this office and you had such a look on your face. You looked like you had seen a ghost."

*I didn't see a ghost, just a total douche-bag.* "I'm fine. Listen, hold my calls. I'm really behind the eight ball with my cases."

She smiled again. "I think that maybe you picked up another one. Santino Bianchi has been waiting to talk to you. He's in the conference room right now."

I groaned. *What did he do now?*

"Do you have time to see him?"

"I guess. I mean, I have a hearing at 1:30, and I have about a million appellate briefs to write and an expert witness coming in, but why not throw something else into the mix?" I felt annoyed, not only because I suspected that good ol' Santino caught yet another case, but also because he just popped in and waited for me. As if I had nothing else to do but help him out again.

I went into the conference room, and Santino was sitting there, his hands clasped in front of him. He saw me come in and stood up and smiled. He went to hug me, and I hugged him back, even though I didn't necessarily want to.

"Miss Serena," he said to me, "you look beautiful as usual. Thanks for seeing me."

I nodded my head but didn't greet him back. "What's

going on?" I narrowed my eyes. "You didn't catch another case did you?"

He shook his head. "No. I'm keeping my nose clean." He touched his nose. "You won't see me in here for another case, I promise." Then he lowered his voice. "I mean, I'm still working for Joey, don't get me wrong. But we're working on making sure that I catch no more cases." He nodded his head and caught his drift – he was still doing shit, but he and Joey were getting better at greasing palms to make sure that nobody ever caught him doing it. I wasn't stupid enough to think that Santino was actually clean.

I sat down. "So, you're here. I hate to give you the bum's rush, but I have a lot going on today. I could schedule you in later on this week, but today looks like a hectic one for me."

"I told you, I don't have another case. I'm here for another reason. A different reason."

I sighed. I didn't want to deal with this. Not today. I just wanted to hide in my office. Hunker down with my files and do my research. Pretend that the world around me doesn't exist. Santino was stepping on this desire, and I resented him thoroughly for it. "Okay, I'll make some time for you. Come on, Santino. Follow me to my office."

Santino beamed like a schoolboy. "Thanks for seeing me on this short notice. I think that you'll be happy that I'm here, though, once you hear what I have to say."

I snarled just a little as Santino followed me into my office. "Have a seat," I said, pointing to the chair that was in front of my desk. "Would you like a cup of coffee?" I went over to my Keurig machine that was in the corner of the office. "You can have any flavor you want, really. Hawaiian Roast, Hazelnut, French Roast, whatever you like."

I didn't really drink a lot of coffee myself, because

caffeine made nauseous, but I kept the machine around because I wanted my clients to feel at home. On this day, though, I felt that coffee was going to get me through this awful day. I put a tiny carton into the machine that was marked French Roast and the machine did its duty.

"I'd like just plain old coffee if you have it. Nothing fancy or nothing like that."

"That can be arranged." I put a little Folger's packet into the machine, and, in no time, there was a cup of coffee that was ready for Santino as well. "Cream and sugar?"

"I drink it black."

"I figured." I gave him the cup and he sipped it while I sat down. "Okay, then, Santino, why don't you tell me what was so urgent for you to drop by like this?" I was aware that I was being rude, but I didn't really care. I was in no mood for any kind of bullshit, and Santino, from what I knew about him, was the absolute King of the bullshit.

He looked around. "This office looks a bit different. Did you do stuff with it?"

I shrugged my shoulders. "I got a new lamp I guess. And a new picture." I pointed to the wall. "I took that picture myself in La Jolla." I was a picture of a cliff with the water rushing up around it. I was proud of that picture, even though I just took it on a cell phone, because I captured the water at just the right time. The sunlight was reflecting, in rays, on the water, and the white peaks were up on the cliff. La Jolla was a beautiful area, anyhow, as it was a place where the seals and sea lions hung out on the rocks and there was a lot of natural rock formations.

Santino nodded at the picture. "It's very nice." He looked at me and took another sip of his coffee.

I just stared at him, trying to figure out what the hell his game was. He wasn't in this office because he wanted to compliment my photography skills or my barista skills, such as they were. "So," I finally said, "to what do I owe this wonderful visit?" I was trying hard to contain my sarcasm, but I knew that I was failing in this.

He shrugged his shoulders. "I don't know. How badly do you want to beat up the Garancinos?"

My ears perked up when he said that. "Why?" I didn't want to give away too much, so I made an effort to seem casual. I remembered that Santino was instrumental in getting Slade off the first time, as he put into motion the chain of events that led me to that video of Malcolm killing Jordan. It was all circuitous, of course, as Santino gave up Michael Garancino, Charlotte's uncle and sometime lover, who wasn't actually guilty of anything. That tip did get me sniffing around the actual culprit, who was Charlotte herself, though, so I owed Santino big-time for that one.

Santino shrugged again. "I just heard that your guy is about to marry Charlotte, I mean Carlotta." He grinned goofily. "You know, I should just call her Carlotta all the time. Charlotte...I mean, could you think of a WASPier name than that? And that dame sure ain't no WASP. Well, unless you could say that she stings you bad for no good reason. Then I guess the term fits."

I was getting impatient and intrigued, both at the same time. I wondered if there was any way that Santino could fit into this whole mess. Take care of Charlotte, bring Slade back...Then I inwardly shrugged. I certainly didn't want to get my hopes up about it. That would do nothing but devastate me further when the whole thing crashed, yet again, like a house of cards.

"He is. Going to marry Charlotte, that is. I mean, Carlotta." I had to smile at Santino's logic of using Charlotte's given name. It suited her much better than the bland name "Charlotte." Well, bland wasn't the right word, but the name did denote a certain type of woman. Like the character of Charlotte on *Sex and the City* – proper, wealthy, mannerly. Carlotta was a name that was clearly Italian, not that that meant anything, but it did bring a different image to mind than did the name "Charlotte."

"So, what do you think about that?"

"Oh, I'm overjoyed," I said sarcastically. "Who wouldn't be when the love of their life goes off to marry a Mafia princess just because said Mafia princess has the ability to have you killed? I mean, really, it's a dream come true for me." I looked at my paperweight and tried mightily to hold back tears. I was trying to be brave about this whole sorry situation, but it was becoming increasingly difficult. My whole life, I was trying to find some kind of security. Something that would moor me. I finally found that with Slade. It was like coming home, really.

And, just like that, it was all snatched away. Which made me start to believe that good things weren't for me. Maybe the only things that were for me in this life were things like work, running, dogs and family. Maybe I wasn't meant to be truly happy with anyone. I could control, however, some things in my life, and those were the things that I chose to focus on. I could work hard, and become the best attorney I could. I could make sure that my family ties were getting stranger. I could make sure that I took care of my health by my daily runs and eating right. I could make sure that Bella and Gigi had the best lives of any dogs.

What I couldn't control was Slade and how he felt about me. I couldn't control Charlotte, either, so I was always in danger that she was going to literally kill me. She certainly was capable of it. I was out of control in those areas of my life, so I had to compartmentalize and simply not think about them. As difficult as it was.

Santino put his hand on mine and looked at me sympathetically. "Well, I heard all about that marriage, and I wanted to throw up. I mean, I ain't go no love for that guy, as he gave me a pretty good beat-down, but I do like you Ms. Serena. I know what it's like to get thrown over like that, believe me. It's happened to me more times than I want to think about."

I smiled and kept trying to hold back the tears. "We've all been there, haven't we, Santino? Our hearts ripped out and stomped on?" The image of a movie I saw long ago, *Indiana Jones and the Temple of Doom,* where the evil savage literally took out the beating heart of the slave, before throwing that slave into a volcano, briefly crossed my mind. That was what I felt like – that slave, with his beating heart ripped out. Hopefully I wouldn't also be sacrificed to a volcano, either literally or figuratively, but one never knows.

"Yes, but Serena, I'd like to help you out here. Whatever I can do."

I had to laugh a little. "Well, thank you, Santino, but I'm not sure what you can do. Besides, I'm okay. I really am. I mean, just look at this desk," I said, sweeping my hand panoramically over the desk, which was piled with files and papers. "I have my work cut out for me, so, you know, I'll be kept busy. As long as I'm busy, I'm okay."

That was wrong, of course. I wasn't okay. Even as I sat across from Santino I felt empty. Like my body was nothing but a shell, encasing a lot of of nothingness. What happens to you when you lose your soul to somebody, and that somebody just ups and leaves, taking your soul with them? You walk around like an empty vessel, devoid of emotion or strength. That's what happens to you. You no longer feel like a human being, but, rather, like an automaton. You feel as if you are among the walking dead. A vampire, maybe, for they no longer have souls either.

Whatever…all that I knew was that I was soulless and dead right at that moment. I would gradually be brought back to life with time. With time. But, right at that moment, there was just a vast nothingness that filled me where life had once been.

"You're not okay." Santino looked at me sympathetically again. "Listen, Vincent Vichelli has a problem with Gianni Garancino, who is the head of that family. He's Carlotta's dad. Gianni is getting on Vincent's turf, again, and the soldiers have been alerted that there might be some kind of war." He leaned a little closer to me. "I would hate it if Carlotta got taken out in the cross-fire, wouldn't you?"

A flicker of hope crossed through my body, and then was extinguished. As much as it sounded good that Charlotte would be a casualty of a Mafia turf war, I didn't have much hope of that happening. And I couldn't ask Santino to be the one who would take her out. I had come to care for Santino in my own way. "Tell me about the turf war," I said to Santino. "And what you were thinking."

Santino opened his mouth, but then my assistant, Anita, came in the door. "I'm so sorry, Serena, but I wanted to alert you to a consultation I scheduled for you with a brand-new client." She lowered her voice. "He kind of has a lot of money, so…" She nodded her head and I got her drift. Our firm might have been infused with Slade cash, but that didn't mean that it was fiscally healthy. Malcolm had left us all in dire straights.

Santino shut his mouth again and stood up. "Listen, maybe this isn't such a good time. I'll be sure and make an appointment with you, though, I promise. Do I talk to Anita to set that up?"

I nodded my head. I was eager to hear what Santino had to say, yet there was a part of me that didn't want to get my hopes up. The situation with Slade was hopeless from the start, and I had always refused to see that. Even if Charlotte were mysteriously killed, then what? Would I be a target of retaliation with that family once they traced her murder back to me, which would surely happen once somebody in that family figures out that I was working with Santino? Would Slade? This whole thing wouldn't be as simple as Santino probably wanted it to be. I knew about Mafia wars, and I wanted no part of it.

Then again, if it could get Charlotte out of the way....

I sighed as Santino left and the new client, one Porter Jones III, walked in. As it turned out, Porter had a will that he wanted to contest, which wasn't necessarily my forte, but was something that I knew a lot about. He was cut out of his grandmother's vast estate for his playboy ways, and he was going to task me to litigate it. Santino, and his little hints at salvation, were long-forgotten as Porter, and one new client after another, streamed through my door. Turned out that all the publicity that I had garnered as being Slade's attorney was finally paying off, and our firm was starting to get its mojo back.

Silver linings....

# Chapter Four

## Slade

I ended up back in San Diego, even though I knew that I couldn't actually see Serena. That would be the death knell for her, I knew, because I wasn't naïve enough to think that Charlotte didn't actually have a bug or a tail that would tell her if I was seeing Serena behind her back. I just wanted to feel closer to her, though. I would be back at work the next day, but, for right now, I just wanted to feel that I was in the same area as the woman I desperately loved.

I went to a little restaurant that was right on the beach, and ordered an omelet and Bloody Mary and watched the people running around outside. It was still a little cool, as it always was in San Diego in the morning, and overcast, which was another typical state of affairs. People always had this image of California in their heads – the image that the sun was always out and the weather was always gorgeous. After all, California was the Golden State, which implied sunshine. But people would be wrong. Overcast weather was relentless in May and June of every year, and then again during the winter months. And, during the summer months, there was plenty of sunshine, but the weather was anything but mild. Blistering hot for days on end was more like it. I had to laugh at one real estate agent's recommendation to me and to any homeowners – if you want to sell your house in California to an out-of-stater, sell it in April. That was one of the only months that wasn't either relentlessly hot or overcast.

Today, then, was a typical California day in November – overcast and cool, but not cold by any means. You could still get in the water, without a wetsuit if you were brave, but there weren't a ton of people doing that. There were still people on the beach, though – running around, building sand castles, playing catch. People on the boardwalk rollerblading with headphones, and bicycling with rented beach cruisers. People walking and running. People...ordinary people.

God, how I craved to be one of those anonymous people. Now that my murder case was a thing of the past, I was becoming one of those anonymous people again. I mean, I was recognized everywhere I went, still, but, since my face was no longer plastered on the 24-hour news channels all the time, I was finding that people were staring at me like a zoo animal much less. In a few more years, I could be one of those people on the boardwalk – non-descript, like everyone else, just running or walking or bicycling, without anyone wanting to take my picture.

Of course, that wasn't going to happen if the inevitable Charlotte wedding went through. That would never happen, and that was one more thing that made me feel like a caged animal in this whole process. She was a big Hollywood star, and was soon going to be huge if word on the street was right. She was determined that I was going to be a part of her power couple. With her talent and my notoriety, we were going to move mountains, according to her. And I would never again be anonymous.

As I sipped my Bloody Mary in this little shack by the beach, I dreamed about what life would be like if I could have my way. I would be married to Serena, and we'd have a few children. Maybe one, maybe two, perhaps three. I'd get out of the LA rat race, and move down here to San Diego. After all, I could bring my company down here and locate its headquarters here. It was much less crowded than LA, and, although it had fewer cultural attractions than LA, it had a certain kind of laid-back charm. I would probably even forgo my enormous mansion and buy a large house in one of the wealthy enclaves like Del Mar. Just a normal house, not some uber mansion with an indoor swimming pool and arcade, like I had up in Malibu.

Serena and I would just do normal things, like go to the zoo with our kids, and take a sailboat out on the weekends. Nothing spectacular, although we'd take trips around the world. That would be the one thing that would be important to me – that my kids be well-rounded. They would have to get to know other cultures and learn other languages. They were going to be a success, and knowing other cultures and languages would help them with that.

I let myself dream for a few minutes before ordering my omelet and home fries. I asked for another Bloody Mary and sat back in my chair. I looked around, and some people were staring and pointing, but, mostly, everyone was enjoying their own food and talking amongst themselves. Nobody seemed to care that notorious billionaire Slade Bridgewell was in their midst, and that was exactly how I liked it.

I fiddled with a napkin, and pondered how in the hell I was going to get out of this mess. I, of course, was going to have to start at the top by getting to know Gianni Garancino, Charlotte's dad and the Garancino crime syndicate head. From what I had always knew, Gianni was secretive and extremely protective of his family. Charlotte, unfortunately, was his "pet," and always had been. That was why she was literally able to get away with murder all those years ago. Why her records were expunged. There were some major strings that were pulled to make sure that Charlotte never had to pay for what she did, and those major strings were pulled by Gianni.

But Gianni might be the key to this whole mess. If anybody was going to rein in Charlotte, it would be him. He would be the person who would be able to call off any future hits, and would be the person who might be able to talk some sense into Charlotte.

I sighed and got my check, and then took a walk along the beach. Then I called Charlotte. "I'm coming back," I told her, being careful not to say the word "home." Charlotte's home wasn't my home, and it never would be.

"I knew that you would be," she said. "Listen, you need to come back right now. I called the paparazzi, and they're going to be staking out our house tonight with some long-range lenses. They're going to be publishing the pictures in the tabloids on Monday. It's very important that this happen tonight."

I simply hung up the phone without saying another word, and then got into my car. I was going to dance like a fucking trained monkey until I figured something out that would protect Serena 100%.

As much as I hated it.

I got back to Charlotte's about 8, and then walked in the door. "Charlotte," I said. "I need to meet with your dad. I'd like to meet with him before we go through with this sham marriage."

Charlotte looked at me suspiciously. "Why?"

"Why not? I mean, we're going to be married. I would think that meeting your dad would be something that would be a prerequisite. Don't you?"

She shook her head. "No. I don't want him getting involved with any of this."

My mind started to turn when she gave me such a weird and evasive answer. "Why not?"

"He doesn't need to, that's all."

I raised an eyebrow. "I need to talk to him."

"You don't."

When she said this, I just decided not to push it. I would meet with Gianni Garancino the first thing the next morning, though. I had a feeling that I finally found her weakness, perhaps her fatal weakness. "Okay. Well, what is it that I need to do right now?"

"Just come out on the terrace and have a meal with me. And hold my hand. That's all."

I shrugged my shoulders. "I guess that's not such a bad thing. That's kind of crazy, though. I can't believe how much manipulation goes into the tabloid stories, although I really shouldn't be." I smiled, thinking that I effortlessly got into the tabloids myself this past year or so. Charlotte had to work for something that just came to me naturally. That's the thing about being wealthy and accused of murder - the tabloid attention just comes with the territory.

We went onto the terrace, and ate dinner. Charlotte

looked around, and then put her hands out. I put my hand on hers and turned my face away. I didn't necessarily think that the picture that was going to be in whatever tabloid was hired to do this nonsense should feature me with a face that showed exactly what I was thinking about this stupid woman.

"So," she said, leaning down. As always, she was wearing a blouse that showed every bit of her assets. Her fingers lightly grazed mine as she stared at me lustfully. I had to suppress the snarl that was threatening to curl my lips. "What is going on with your current criminal case?"

"Jackson is working with the prosecutors. It looks like I'm going to have to be on probation for a few years." I had to admit that this was an excellent result, but I knew that Jackson would work miracles for me. I was facing a felony charge, but Jackson had told me that I was going to be pleading to a misdemeanor of mishandling a corpse, and would never see the inside of a jail cell. I would have to pay a fine, of course, but that wasn't a big deal at all. Whatever the fine was, I was going to gladly pay it. I never wanted to think about that case again. After all, this was the case that put this whole sorry scenario into motion. If mom didn't kill that guy, or if Charlotte wasn't present when Hugh's dead body was on the floor, then none of the sorry mess that happened to me would have happened.

Then again, maybe I wouldn't have met Serena if the circumstances were different. That made all of what I went through worth it to me. 100%.

Charlotte nodded. "That's a wonderful thing. It really wouldn't do for you to be behind bars, you know."

"I know." I cleared my throat and tried to tackle my food again. I took a deep breath and just stared at Charlotte. There was nothing to say. I had nothing in common with her, and just being in her presence revolted me. I just wanted to get out of there as quickly as I could, but I knew that I couldn't just yet. After all, there was the matter of the two of us sleeping in the same bed that night.

I could only hope that, if Charlotte and I ended up in the same bed that night, it would the last time that would happen. I was going to get out of this situation as quickly as I could.

And I was starting to find out just how that was going to happen.

---

That night, as I lay in bed with Charlotte, I finally got the answer that I was maybe looking for. It was a text from Serena. I didn't want communication with her, not until I knew everything was safe, so I hated that she texted me. Yet, at the same time, I loved it. I craved having communication with her, any kind of communication.

"Slade," the text began, "I didn't want to bother you, but Santino Bianchi stopped by my office today. I've been thinking about it more and more, and he says that he has information that might help you. Something about a turf war between the Garancinos and the Vichellis. Word is the Vichellis are the more powerful family of the two. Maybe this will help."

My heart quickened. This immediately started the wheels turning in my head. Charlotte was snoring beside me, and I crept silently out of bed. I went into the adjoining room, which was furnished as an office for Charlotte, and booted up the computer. I pulled up some articles about the Vichellis and the Garancinos, and it was clear to me, after reading the news articles, that Serena was right. If you read between the lines, it was clear that the Vichellis were getting the better of the Garancinos. The Vichellis appeared to control more real estate and more "legitimate" businesses. They also seemed to have a bigger stake in the Vegas casinos. They had more ways to launder their money, and it seemed that they had many more assets than the Garancinos.

Something told me that this just might be the key to solving my living hell.

# Chapter Five

## Serena

I had to admit that, after I really had a chance to think about Santino's visit, I started to think about things. Maybe he did have something to tell me. Perhaps his information was going to be relevant. I shouldn't have dismissed it, and, if I were in a better frame of mind, I probably wouldn't have. So, I decided to go ahead and call him.

"Miss Serena," he said as he picked up the phone. "To what do I owe this honor?"

"Santino, I need to talk to you. Can you meet me out somewhere?"

"Come to my restaurant after-hours. I'll cook you an amazing Italian meal and we can share some wine and some laughs. Break bread together."

"Okay." I hesitated, remembering that Santino had hit on me the last time we were alone together. "But Santino…"

"Don't worry, Miss Serena. I'm a married man now.

Well, not married, but I kind of have an old lady now. Maybe she'll be Mrs. Bianchi one day. So, I only want to meet with you as a plutonic thing."

I smiled, thinking that he invented a new word – plutonic. Santino tended to get his words mixed up anyhow, as when he used to call the prosecutor a "persecutor." Then again, maybe that was intentional. Sometimes a prosecutor seems like a persecutor. Probably seemed that way to Santino quite a bit.

"Okay," I said, "it'll be platonic. What time can we meet?"

"Seven tonight will be good. I'll reserve a booth where we can have some privacy."

"See you then."

As I got off the phone I wondered if there was any way that Santino might actually give me the opening that I needed to get Slade out of his arrangement with Charlotte. Could it really be as easy as meeting with this mobster? Might he be the missing piece of the puzzle?

I texted Slade, knowing that I was putting myself in danger for doing that. But I had to let him know that there was a trail now that we could follow. This trail might lead us to where we need to go. It might be premature, but if I could put the bug in his ear about Santino's tip, and I could work independent with Santino on this end, maybe, just maybe, the two ends could meet and we could have a plan worked out. All without explicitly collaborating, because that would just mean that Slade and I would be in danger. Charlotte must never get wind of any of this, of course.

That evening, I met Santino in his restaurant. As usual, it was bustling. He had a piano player that night, and I heard standard after standard while the people in the restaurant cheered. I smiled, because I loved the standards. There was something about forties love songs that were so heartfelt and gorgeous. They made me imagine old movies, where the men wore hats and the leggy women always wore dresses and perpetually had a pout. They were dames, really, in every sense of the word. Dames in that they were classic, and dames because that's what the wise-guys called them. There were times that I wished that I could have lived in that era, and there was a part of me that felt like maybe I did. Indeed, I had dreams about living in that era, which made me think that there was a part of my soul that had lived back then, and I was reincarnated into the person that I was right now. And I would reincarnated again once I shuffled off this mortal coil.

The piano player started playing *Smoke Gets In Your Eyes*, and I swayed deftly to the music. Santino, for his part, was bustling around, giving me signals that he would be with me as soon as he could make some time. I wasn't necessarily in a hurry, though. I mean, I was, because I was so anxious to hear what Santino had to say. At the same time, however, I was enjoying myself. I was enjoying listening to the music and I was enjoying watching the crowd. My stomach was rumbling, though, and I knew that I was soon going to have to eat.

Santino finally broke away. "Sorry Miss Serena," he said, "things just got really busy and I had to pitch in with the wait staff." He shook his head. "Somebody called in sick, so I fear that this little dinner is going to have to be a short one. But follow me over to that booth." He pointed at a booth at the far end of the restaurant. It was in a station that was closed off to the public, so I knew that we wouldn't be interrupted.

"Thanks," I said, following him over.

We sat down and Santino snapped his fingers. A waitress came over, and we ordered. I just got spaghetti with marinara sauce, as that was really the only thing that I could eat on the menu, and Santino ordered lasagna. "And garlic bread made with olive oil," he said, winking at me. "Right Serena? You can't have butter." He nodded, as if he was proud to have remembered that I didn't consume animal products.

"Very good," I said to Santino. "You have a good memory."

"Of course I do. I mean, I might be a goombah, but I try to always remember certain things about the ladies." He lowered his voice. "That's what gets them more than anything, you know. To know stuff about them. Act concerned. At least, that's how my momma always taught me."

I had to laugh a little bit at that one. I wondered what Santino's momma looked like. I had the stereotypical Italian woman in my head, although I had no idea if it was accurate or not. I imagined her to be busty and big, with black hair with grey stripes throughout. Heavy eyebrows and a large nose. I pictured her standing over a pot of spaghetti, literally stirring the pot. I wondered how on the money I was.

Santino seemed to read my mind, which amused me, because usually I was the one reading minds. "Here's my momma," he said, bringing out his wallet.

I was impressed, for his momma looked nothing like I would have pictured her. She was a petite woman, maybe 100 lbs, with fair skin and green eyes. Her hair was black, although there wasn't a grey stripe through it. She didn't look very old, and I wondered if this was an old picture.

"She's pretty," I said, looking at her. "When was this picture taken?"

"Just two years ago." He looked proud. "My momma tries to keep in shape. It's hard for her, though, because she does love her pasta."

"Is she from the old country?"

"She is. So is my pops. And Joey." He smiled. "But I'm sure that you didn't meet me here to hear all about my family tree. You want to know what I know about the Garancinos."

"I do." I leaned forward, and the waitress came around and brought our bread. Santino looked at me and pointed.

"You want some wine?"

I shook my head. I felt like this was almost a business dinner, so I didn't necessarily know if drinking wine was such a good idea. "I'm driving."

"I'll call you a limo to take you home."

"No, really, that's okay." I cleared my throat. "I'd just like a water."

Santino shook his head. "Okay. Well, I'll be drinking wine. I hope that you don't mind that."

"Of course not."

He ordered a glass of Chianti, and some more water for me. "Okay, then, Miss Serena, let's get down to business here. Like I said in your office, I know about what's going on with Carlotta and Slade. And, Miss Serena, I really think that you deserve to be happy a little. So I'd like to help."

I leaned forward again and played with a napkin. "Santino, I really appreciate you meeting me here. I know that you're sticking your neck out to come and talk to me like this, so I wanted you to know that it's not going unnoticed."

"Of course Miss Serena." It was his turn to lean down. "Okay, well, here's what's going on. There's a deal going down involving some white powder coming up from Mexico. Maybe the people in Mexico want to sell the stuff to the Garancinos in exchange for some high-powered arms. The Garancinos are armed to the teeth, let me tell you what. But maybe Vincent Vichelli wants to try to stop that deal from going through." Santino looked around the restaurant. "Maybe this deal is such a high-level deal that it's going to change the nature of the game, if you know what I mean. The Garancinos need to control a few more assets around this town and around Vegas in order for them to get the jump on Vincent and his team."

I nodded my head. I wondered where this was going, and if I could use it to get Slade out of this whole mess. "Go on."

"Maybe that little number Carlotta is trying to screw with this whole thing." His voice got low. "She hates her father. Bet you didn't know that. Her father got Michael Garancino killed. You know, Carlotta's uncle. Word is she's trying to change that Mexican dealer's mind. Name's Miguel Sanchez. She's using her assets to double-cross her own dad so that Miguel puts the deal through with the Vichellis, not with the Garancinos."

My heart quickened. "Her…"

"Her own father will have her killed if he knew what was going on there. There's your ace in the hole."

I pondered Santino's words. Her own father would have her killed if he knew what was going on there. "How does Gianni Garancino not know all this?"

"Blind spot. He's nave when it comes to Carlotta, you know?"

I suppressed a smile when Santino used the word

"nave," when he clearly meant "naïve." There was a little bit of Archie Bunker in this guy sometimes. "So, how do I make him believe that she's screwing him like this?"

Santino sat back and I closed my eyes. I had to tune into his vibrations to see if Santino was pulling a fast one on me. Not that he would have a reason to do so, but one just never knows. I couldn't believe this information was falling into my lap, and I just didn't trust it. But I didn't feel any deception coming from him, so I calmly decided just to let him continue. Inside, though, my mind was turning. "What do you suggest?"

Santino shook his head. "There's no love lost between Gianni and Carlotta. It probably wouldn't take much for Slade to convince him that Carlotta is a rat."

I took a deep breath, and then took a sip of my water. Inside, my stomach was rumbling and I felt like I was going to be sick. I didn't know why I felt that way, except that this information was settling in. I should have been elated, though, not feeling nauseated.

Maybe I was feeling sick because I suddenly saw what a dangerous game was about to be opened up. Playing Slade against Charlotte, with Gianni Garancino in the middle? And getting a Mexican drug dealer involved with it all? What, Slade was just supposed to put a bug in Gianni's ear about Charlotte double-crossing him, and all was supposed to be well? And what kind of proof was going to be needed about this whole thing? What was Charlotte giving this Miguel dude to go over to the Vichellis? There were so many unanswered questions, and I just had to wait for the answers. But I was growing impatient waiting, even though the conversation was moving along at a lightning-quick speed.

"I don't understand," I finally said to Santino. Although

I was getting any deception vibrations from him, that didn't mean that he didn't mean this whole thing wasn't bullshit. He might honestly believe it to be true. Santino wasn't the sharpest tool in the box, after all. "Why would this Miguel listen to Charlotte?"

"Sanchez has all the cards here. Word is that his drug shipment is one of the biggest ever. No shit. And he's evenly split between who he's going to deal with. Whoever gets it gets the whole enchilada, you know what I mean? One family after another has tried to deal with him, and he's down to the Garancinos and the Vichellis. And he don't know who he'll go with. So, Carlotta is trying some extra persuasion to get him to make the right choice. The Vichellis."

I raised an eyebrow. "Santino, I guess I don't understand why you're talking to me about this. If I do something, and the drugs go to the Garancinos because of my actions, you don't get anything out of this. Right?"

Santino, to my surprise, shrugged. " I'd really like to get that little Carlotta bitch myself." He raised his own eyebrows. "She killed my teacher." Then he lowered his eyes, and, to my surprise, I saw tears. "My teacher who was also my first love."

I put my hand on his and closed my eyes. Grief was pouring out of him and was flooding me. Santino was telling the truth about this, but still…it seemed like this was a dangerous game for him too. If Vincent Vichelli found out that Santino was meddling in this huge transaction, in an attempt to tip it to the Garancinos…I shuddered to think what might happen to him. One thing was for sure, I was going to have to tread lightly on this one. Perhaps was I was a little hasty in naming Santino in my text to Slade. Not that Slade would give up Santino in this whole mess. But he was going to have to say where he got this information for it to be credible.

So many layers to think about on this one. I honestly had no idea where to start. "I'm very sorry to hear about your teacher," I said to him softly. "I know what it's like to lose the person you love."

He shook his head. "You lost Slade I guess, but that's not the same. You'll get him back. I can never do the same with Rachel."

Rachel? That wasn't the name of the person who Charlotte was named as killing. That must have meant that she killed another teacher, a different one. I shook my head. I shouldn't have been surprised, but I kinda was. Charlotte was proving to be even more of a psycho than I already thought. "I lost Slade, but you're right. There's hope for us. But I did lose my mother violently." I told Santino the story of my mother at that fateful McDonald's, and he listened and shook his head.

"Fucking psychos. If they're suicidal, they should just kill themselves. Why take down a bunch of others on the way?"

I shook my head and looked down at my food. I twirled some spaghetti around my spoon, and thought about Santino's words. All of them. There was a plan, maybe, that could permanently drive a wedge between Charlotte and her dad, which could, possibly, mean that I could be safe. I wouldn't imagine that a hit could come unless her dad ordered it, and I would imagine that, even if Charlotte tried to get somebody else involved with the hit, her dad could stop it cold. That wouldn't mean that Charlotte herself wouldn't try to kill me or have me killed, but it would be easier to evade her than to evade an entire network of people.

We'd still be playing a dangerous game, but it would be slightly less dangerous than before. That was something to hold onto. A glimmer of hope. I'd have to find a way to meet with Slade, and I knew that wasn't going to be easy. Charlotte probably put every tracking device known to man on Slade, so he was going to have to think this whole thing through.

I decided to send him another text. I had no idea if Charlotte had real-time access to his texts, but I had to do something. "Hold off and don't mention Santino. We need to meet, and soon." That's all the text said. And then I added "our place 8 tomorrow." Slade knew that "our place" referred to this tiny bar that was right on the beach, facing the boardwalk. We used to go there whenever he would stay with me at my home. He loved going there because it made him feel normal. Nobody bothered him there, and he could have a drink and relax and not worry about anybody pointing at him.

I didn't get a text back from him, but I didn't obsess about that. It was entirely possible that Charlotte would know if he sent a text, even if she didn't necessarily know that there was one incoming. How that would be, I wasn't sure, but I knew one thing.

I was going to be seeing Slade, and soon.

Santino and I talked some more about Miguel. He assured me that if I wanted to see Miguel, I could. I just had to call Santino, and he would be the intermediary between us. He told me where Miguel lived, too. After talking with Santino, I started to feel hopeful that maybe, just maybe, there could be a plan that might work after all.

## Chapter Six

The next day, I found out another incredible thing. Turns out that Derek was fired. Anita, my assistant, came into my office as I was working on yet another appellate brief. I had noticed that Derek had been gone from the office, but I didn't care enough to ask why. He was dead to me, as far as I was concerned, so why should I care if a dead person shows up to work or not?

Yet, when Anita told me that news, my heart soared. "Derek is gone," she said to me after she came into my office. "And the rumor is that you have something do with it."

I gave Anita a look, trying to figure out if she was accusing me or simply stating a fact. I closed my eyes and decided that it was the latter. "I might have had something to do with it. Why? What have you heard?"

"That you and he had bad blood. At any rate, firing him was a decision that came straight from the top. Meaning Mr. Bridgewell." She cocked her head at me. "That would imply that you probably did have something do with it."

I took a deep breath and shrugged my shoulders. I wasn't feeling like talking to Anita about this, although I was inwardly overjoyed. "Why do you say that?"

"Well, I guess…" Her voice trailed off. "Maybe not. I mean, I don't want to step out of line, but you and Mr. Bridgewell were together. Now I'm hearing that he's dating Charlotte Boswell. I read that in the papers today. It's so weird." Her face turned red. "If you ever need to talk about that, I'll listen and not judge. I've always liked you, Ms. Roberts."

My heart sunk. The "dating" between Slade and Charlotte already made the papers? Which papers?

The masochist in me sprung forth, unbidden, and couldn't stop what was going to be my next request from poor Anita. "What papers?"

She left without a word, and, not five minutes later, came back in. She showed me a tabloid with a picture of Slade and Charlotte sitting on a terrace, his hand on hers. She was looking at him with a expression that told the camera man that she was head over heels. His face was turned away, so I couldn't see his expression. It was clear, though, that this picture was one that wasn't posed or staged. It seemed to be a completely natural picture that was taken with a long-range lens.

I felt tears coming to my eyes as I read the story. "Charlotte Boswell, the current 'It' girl in Hollywood, has publicly denied a relationship with the notorious billionaire playboy, Slade Bridgewell, but exclusive photos taken in the star's Malibu home tell a different story. Readers might remember that, up until recently, Mr. Bridgewell was under suspicion of a brutal murder. Now that he's beaten this rap, it seems that he wants to take another title – the King of Hollywood.

He'll prove that by canoodling with the current Queen, Charlotte Boswell."

I stopped reading after that. It wasn't just the corny prose, although that kind of made me want to hurl as well. It was more the fact that the story was accompanied by an intimate picture of the two of them. I fully expected to see posed pictures of them out and about. What I didn't expect was to see a picture of them at Charlotte's house, having a romantic dinner, with his hand covering hers. Granted, I couldn't see his face in the picture, but I didn't have to. Just seeing his hand covering hers was enough to devastate me.

"This is a rag," I said, throwing the paper in disgust at Anita. "Don't bother me with this again."

"I won't," she said. "But I'd like to know what happened. I mean, we all kinda thought…"

"What? That Slade and I would be the ones getting married? Whatever would make you think that?"

"We saw the two of you at Malcolm's funeral, and nobody could look at a woman like Slade looked at you and not think that a marriage isn't pending at some time soon."

"Well, you obviously thought wrong. Looks like Slade is going to be the King of Hollywood." I snorted. "I guess that's what he deserves. To continue to be hounded by photographers for the rest of his life." My voice got louder, as I started to feel that I was getting out of control. "Bastard. He could have chosen to live a quiet life with me. All that publicity would have died down as soon as he got boring. But no. He decides to live life in the spotlight, just as he always has. Well, he won't coming whining to me about how his life isn't his own. I'll tell him where to go."

It was then that I looked at Anita, who was sitting there in a chair, her eyes downcast. I hadn't realized that I had just said all that out loud, in front of my assistant, and I immediately felt embarrassed and unprofessional. "Oh, I'm sorry...."

She shook her head. "Trust me, we've all been there. Screwed over by some charming jerk. What woman hasn't experienced that?"

I had to smile. She had a point. If a woman is still dating people at a certain age, and not yet happily married, she's going to experience more than her share of douchebags along the way. It certainly comes with the territory of trying to find the right person.

And I thought that Slade was that right person....

It was then that I made my decision. I was going to bring down Charlotte, but I wasn't going to involve Slade. He didn't deserve to work with me. I wanted my revenge on that bitch, but I wasn't going to allow Slade back into my life.

As far as I was concerned, he was as dead to me as Derek.

## Chapter Seven

I made my decision. I was going to go to Mexico and find this Miguel Sanchez person and I was going to talk to him myself. I was going to involve Slade in this whole operation, but, after seeing that picture in the paper, I decided that Slade wasn't going to come with me after all. Fuck him. He deserved to show up at that little bar on the beach and find that I wasn't there. Let him make a trip down to San Diego for nothing. And let him go to my house and find that I wasn't there, either. Neither were Bella and Gigi – they were put into a doggie hotel for the time being.

A part of me was screaming that I was making the wrong decision. A wrong decision that just might get me killed. It was a stupid decision, too, really. But there was another part of me that felt reckless. Maybe there was a little bit of a death-wish in there. Because one thing was for sure – seeing that picture of Slade and Charlotte didn't just make me want to throw up.

It made me want to die.

And what better way to die than at the hands of a

Mexican drug dealer who was most likely armed to the teeth and paranoid as hell? Santino gave me all the information that I would need to find this guy, which was mistake number one. He had offered to come with me, but I refused, which was mistake number two. There were sure to be other mistakes, but I didn't really care.

What I cared about was that I was going to get the evidence that I needed to nail Charlotte to the wall with her own family. If I didn't get that evidence, I'd probably end up dead, which was fine, too. Either way, things were going to be better, because they were going to be different. That was literally all that I knew at that point.

I drove down to Mexico right after work, and, since the Mexican border was only about twenty minutes away from my office, it didn't take me long to get there. I got into the line of cars at the border, streaming into Mexico as the workers filed into that country after their own long days at work. That was what it was like in San Diego – there were quite a few people who worked in the city and went home each evening to Mexico. It was the best of both worlds for them – they got the relatively high wage in San Diego, and then went down to their families in Tijuana, where the cost of living was exceedingly low. I thought that these enterprising Mexican people probably lived like Kings and Queens down there, even if they made the minimum wage in San Diego. In a city where people lived on five dollars a day, making even $7.50 per hour was more than a living wage.

The border city was San Ysidro, and, right at the border, was a veritable treasure trove of small shops and bazaars. I had come down here before, from time to time, shopping at the colorful booths. There was anything that anybody could ever want, and it was all cheap. Sure, the "designer" purses weren't exactly designer, as they might have had the words "Fendi" on them, but they sure as hell weren't quality made. The "saltwater pearls" were most likely plastic, carefully crafted to fool the most discerning customer. Etc. But that didn't matter to the hoards of people who lined the streets, looking for bargains and often finding them. To them, just having a purse with the Fendi name was enough.

While the border town had a carnival atmosphere, I knew that, once I crossed the border, I'd have a tougher time. Down there, people led you into their shops by your hand. The men would stand outside the shop and actually come up to you and physically take you into the shop so that you could buy something. Walk down the streets in the touristy part of the city, and you'll be hassled to come into bars and try free tequila. But Tijuana wasn't so bad, considering its reputation. I wasn't at all concerned, because the bars and shops down there always seemed to be filled with Americans eager to be parted from their weekly salaries. Indeed, since Tijuana was so close to San Diego, there were also plenty of Americans who went down there to get dental work done on the cheap, or get a pair of eyeglasses or seek a solution to any number of medical or dental issues. I felt comfortable coming to TJ, as Tijuana was colloquially called.

But Miguel didn't live in Tijuana, of course. He lived in Ciudad Juarez, in the Chihuahua peninsula in central Mexico, right on the Texas border. Ciudad Juarez was where the powerful drug cartel, the Jalisco New Generation Cartel, CJNG for short, ruled with an iron fist. The CJNG used military-style weapons in its constant battle with law enforcement, and used these same weapons with rival crime networks. They specialized, in addition to drug smuggling, cooking and running, in kidnapping, extortion and murder. I wasn't quite prepared to meet with Miguel, and I wouldn't be until I purchased a gun, which wouldn't be at all difficult to do in Tijuana. That was my plan, such as it was – go to Tijuana and get a gun and talk to some locals about Ciudad Juarez. Get some information about it. And then just go on down there and find Miguel and try to get some information from him about the deals he was making with both the Vichellis and the Garancinos. I was going to get a recording of him telling me that Charlotte was the one who was trying to manipulate him into going with the Vichellis over the Garancinos, and if I died doing this, I died.

If I lived, and I got that recording, then I'd have the ammunition that I would need to get Charlotte gone. Her father would either banish her or have her killed. Either way, my life would be spared. I really didn't care what happened with that bitch, either. Her life was like a bug on a windshield to me. It was of no consequence.

Fuck Slade. I had no idea what his plan was, and I didn't fucking care. This was my plan, and, even though it was beyond dangerous, I was going to do it.

But the first thing that I had to do, before I did anything else, was to get a TracPhone. I didn't want Slade tracking my movements once I got over the border. I was that infuriated with him. I wanted to do this whole operation completely on my own.

It was then that I realized that maybe I really did have a death-wish. Losing Slade was the last straw, and I had to come to terms with that in my psyche. Perhaps I was going just a little bit crazy, and, really, if you think about it, I deserved to go nuts. All my life, I had to endure one tragedy after another. I tried, so hard, to keep it all together, and it was always difficult. Then, I met Slade, and things started to finally make sense. It seemed that I was finally turning a corner in my life.

Then he dumped me, and, more importantly, he lied to me. He fucking lied to me. He made it seem like he was with Charlotte for one reason, and that was to buy some time so that he could find a way for us to be together. Well, that picture of him, that candid, intimate picture of him, holding Charlotte's hand, said otherwise. It wasn't a posed picture. It was something that was taken by a photographer that Slade had to be completely unaware of.

I swallowed hard, absolute fury wracking through my body. The line of cars were moving slowly, too slowly. I knew why – it was rush hour, really, for all the Mexican people who worked in San Diego, along with the San Diegans and other Americans who were eager to get down to TJ and have some cheap or free tequila. I laid my arm down on my arm rest in the car, and cursed silently. Traffic jams, which happened far too often in this city anyhow, always made me extremely impatient. At this moment, with how I was feeling, this traffic jam was making me feel a little bit nuts.

I finally got to the border, where the agent asked me what I was doing, where I was going and when I would be back.

"I'm going down to Tijuana," I said, trying to be as pleasant as possible. "To go to a restaurant to meet some friends. I plan to stay overnight, and will be back in the States tomorrow morning."

The agent just nodded his head and I went on through. It was my experience that it was fairly easy to get over the border. Coming back from Mexico was the trickier part, because that was when the drug-sniffing dogs got involved. Obviously, people going into Mexico were less likely to be up to no good - smuggling drugs or people – then the people coming out of Mexico, so the border agents didn't give the Americans much hassle when they wanted to leave.

Not that I was going to have any issues coming back into the States, unless, of course, Miguel asked me to do something for him in exchange for any information he was going to give me. I thought of that, too – maybe Miguel would tell me about Charlotte in exchange for my bringing drugs back into America or something like that. In which case, I didn't quite know what I was going to do. Getting Charlotte was officially an obsession with me, ever since I saw that picture. At that moment, I was prepared to do anything, anything at all, in order to see her fry.

There was a voice that was talking to me, as voices sometimes do, whenever I was about to make a huge mistake. I used to think that it was the voice of my guardian angel, and there were occasions when I still thought that. I knew that I had an angel watching over me – I had seen her on more than one occasion. I swear I saw her after my mother was killed, and she stopped me from doing anything rash then. And then again after Derek raped me, and I wanted to kill him – she stopped me from doing so.

Now, she was speaking to me, and saying things clearly. I chose to ignore her this time, though.

"*Serena,*" she was saying. "*You have to go back. This isn't the path that you're supposed to be on.*"

I shook my head. "Go away," I snarled. "I've had enough. I'm at my breaking point, and I'm going to get that bitch, even if I have to die trying."

I turned up the radio on full blast so that I wouldn't have to hear her, and that seemed to do the trick. She was going to tell me all kinds of bullshit about how I shouldn't be doing this, blah, blah, blah, and I simply didn't want to hear it.

With tears in my eyes, I went to the first pawn shop I found and purchased a gun and a TracPhone. I turned in my iPhone and was given $100 USD for it. I was careful to erase the phone and upload all my pictures and contacts and everything important onto the cloud before I did all this.

"Senora," the man behind the counter said to me. "You're trading in your iPhone for a TracPhone?" He shook his head. He probably knew that I was up to no good, because nobody in their right mind would trade in their smart phone for a TracPhone unless they were up to no good. "Whatever you're planning, be careful."

I furled my brow and held out my hand for my money and said nothing. Then I shook my head as he counted out the $100. My guardian angel was probably speaking through this guy, which was another trick that she tried to play when I wouldn't listen to her. "Thanks," I simply said, as I made my way out the door.

The next stop was a motel, and I checked in and laid down on the bed. I tried, hard, to stop my racing thoughts, but I couldn't. Was I finally, at long last, cracking up? Was that picture of Slade the final straw? Was my sanity going to be gone in the morning? Was it gone now?

I didn't know. I didn't really want to know. I needed to complete this mission, such as it was, and I needed to complete it soon.

Either Charlotte was going to be exiled or dead or I would be. Either way, it would be a change.

And change is always good, right?

# Chapter Eight

## Slade

Serena left me this text message to meet her, and I was getting ready to, when I checked my phone. There was something that was telling me, a little voice inside of me, that was telling me that Serena wasn't going to be where she said she was going to be. My instinct caused me to check my tracker for her, and I immediately saw that she was over the Mexican border, and that was where the trail ended.

I knew what happened at that moment, although I wasn't sure exactly why. She had chosen to go to Mexico, as opposed to meeting with me, and she apparently decided to get rid of her phone someplace in Tijuana. Unfortunately, the tracking device simply said that she was in Tijuana, and I couldn't pinpoint exactly where she was right at that moment.

"Goddammit," I said, looking at my tracker. "What the fuck is she doing?"

I was going to take the chance to meet with Serena,

even though I knew that Charlotte was tracking me, too, or, at least, I suspected that she was. Bug sweeps of my car had so far turned up nothing, but I didn't trust her one bit.

At the moment, Charlotte wasn't at home. She was on the set of her new movie, and she had told me that morning not to expect her home until at least midnight. I thought that was perfect, because I'd meet with Serena to get a plan together, hoping that Charlotte wasn't tracking me, and then I'd rapidly carry out whatever plan Serena and I would come up with. Whatever it was, it would involve my going straight to Gianni, Charlotte's father, and try to play the father against the daughter. I needed some leverage, though, and I had hoped that Serena and I could come up with exactly what this leverage was going to be.

Yet Serena had other plans, and I had no clue on what these other plans were. She was in Tijuana, somewhere, and I needed to find a way to figure out just where she was going.

So, I called Santino's restaurant. Obviously, Santino was going to be able to direct me on where Serena was, or where she was going. He was the key to this whole thing, really. Santino was the person who told Serena something important about Charlotte, and I needed to find out just what that something was.

A pleasant-sounding woman answered the phone. "Santino's Restaurant, how may I help you?"

"Yes, is Santino in tonight?"

"No, I'm sorry, he has the night off."

I shook my head. I had no idea how to get ahold of him, other than call his restaurant. I obviously never bothered to get his cell phone number or his address from Serena, because I never thought that to be relevant. I did know where he worked, though, and that was my one life-line. "Could you tell me when he is expected back?"

"He took a few days off, but he'll be back on Monday."

Monday? Today was Thursday. I couldn't wait that long to find out where the hell Serena went. "I really need to speak with him as soon as possible." I took a deep breath, wondering what I could tell this woman that would convince her to tell me where I could find Santino.

"Well, I'm very sorry," she said, "but he went to his house in Italy for a few days. You'll just have to call back on Monday."

Italy? Who goes to Italy on a whim for a few days? Mobsters, that's who. He probably had some important business over there. Somebody needed to be bumped off no doubt.

I bit my lower lip. All this technology I had, and it was useless to me at that moment. Serena was somewhere in Mexico, I had no idea why, and I had no clue where. She was up to something, and I needed to find out immediately what exactly that something was.

She was in danger. That much I knew.

I took a deep breath. I was going to have to go down there and try to charm this hostess, or whomever she was, in person. I was going to have to find out just where Santino was, or get his cell phone number, or something. I needed to speak with him, because only he knew exactly what was going down with Serena.

"Okay," I finally said.

Then I got in my car and flew down to San Diego. I drove as fast as I possibly could, because I not only had to get down there before that restaurant closed, but I also knew that time was of the essence.

Somehow, I knew, in my heart, that if I didn't reach Serena soon, it was going to be too late.

---

I got to Santino's restaurant, and immediately went in there. "Hi," I said to the pretty hostess who looked at me with a sly smile. "My name is Slade Bridgewell, I, well, I have to find out where Santino is tonight."

She batted her eyelashes coyly and blushed. "I knew that I recognized you," she said with a little giggle. "Do you need a table?"

I leaned down on the lectern, where she kept her menus and tried to turn on the charm offensive. "I do," I said in a low voice. "But I really need to find Santino. It's business." I nodded to her knowingly. I had no idea if she knew what Santino did on the side. Looking at her, I thought that she probably didn't. She looked pretty naïve.

She cocked her head. "Are you a supplier? If you are, I can put you in touch with the purchasing manager. I mean, Santino usually does the purchasing, except for when he's out of town, of course. Which he is. He's at his home in Palermo."

*Now I was getting somewhere.* "Palermo. Does he go there often?"

She giggled again. I was surprised that Santino would have a hostess who was so not-savvy about exactly what he did when he wasn't at that restaurant. If I were Santino, and I was watching my back, I'd make sure that all my employees knew never to say a word about me when I wasn't around. But this little girl, who couldn't be more than 16, obviously wasn't instructed about all that.

"Well, yes," she said. "I mean, there's another Santino's

there. He doesn't have much part in it, though. He's mainly a silent partner. But I know that he likes to visit that restaurant from time to time. You know, kinda pop in unexpectedly, see how things are running there."

*Bingo.* I was amazed at how easy this was.

No, it was simple, not easy. Easy would be actually getting Santino's phone number and just calling him. Easy would be if Santino actually was at the other Santino's in Palermo, and I could just call the restaurant and talk to him.

Somehow, I knew that this mission wasn't going to be that easy.

I tried, for about another thirty minutes, to get more out of this hostess. The restaurant wasn't busy, so she as able to talk to me pretty freely. Try as I might, though, I couldn't get her to tell me his cell number.

So, that was it. I was going to have to fly to Palermo that night. I couldn't risk just calling the restaurant the next day, only to have them tell me that he wasn't expected in. And I couldn't risk him not wanting to talk to me over the phone, even if he was in his Santino's restaurant in Palermo. After all, he wouldn't necessarily believe me if I told him who I was, and he probably didn't want to give those sensitive details over the phone.

After I left Santino's, I immediately went to the airport and got my private plane, calling my pilot on the way. "Alex," I said, getting him out of bed, no doubt. He tended to go to bed early because he had to be up at 5 AM most mornings for work. "I'm sorry for the short notice, but I need you to take me to Sicily tonight," I said. "I'll contact your regular boss and tell him what's going on, so he can find a substitute for you for the next day or so."

"Okay," he said. "I'll meet you at the airport in a half hour."

Good ol' Alex. I could always count on him to save me in a pinch.

This was a desperate time, so, of course, it called for desperate measures.

Damn Serena, though. Why would she do such a thing? How could she be so stupid? I just knew that she was down there trying to find out something that she could use against Charlotte. What that thing was, I didn't necessarily know. Santino knew, though, and I was determined that he was going to tell me exactly what that was.

# Chapter Nine

## Serena

The next day, I felt more well-rested, but I still was bound and determined to go through with my plan. The first thing that I needed to do was get a regular map of Mexico. I had never ventured further than Tijuana, with the one exception of the time I took a cruise to the Florida Keys and Cozumel. That was going to tell me nothing, though, of course. The only thing that I remember about that cruise was that I was drinking a lot, and that the water was beautiful. But that was strictly a tourist thing – I did the whole Carlos and Charlie's thing, which apparently was mandatory in Cozumel, and drank plenty of cheap tequila.

This trip, of course, was going to be completely different. I knew just where to go to find this Miguel, as Santino had filled me in on it before he left my house. And, if I could use my GPS, I'd find his house no problem. But I, of course, wasn't going to use my GPS, because I figured that

Slade would be able to find me if I did. I was bound and determined that I was going to do this on my own.

My inner voice was bugging me. First it was the guardian angel, now it was my inner voice. "Why don't you let Slade help you at least?" the voice asked.

"Because I don't want his help anymore. I don't want him around me. I hate him. He killed me. Ripped out my soul, and then lied to me. Lied to me. Told me that he was only with Charlotte to gather information, and then apparently held her hand behind closed doors. I want revenge on Charlotte, and I want him to leave me the hell alone."

There, that should answer that nagging goddamned voice.

I went to a local drug store and purchased a map of Mexico, including all the highways that would take me to the Chihuahua province, and then onto Ciudad Juarez. Once I got into Ciudad Juarez, I would simply get a map that would show me the street names and find this place where Miguel lived. Santino told me that Miguel lived in a veritable fortress that is high on a hill, and that, if I wanted to go and see Miguel, Santino would call him to make sure that I would be able to get in to see him.

I called Santino's cell phone. He picked up right away. "Hello?" he asked. I, frankly, was surprised that he picked up the phone, considering I was using a random phone and he couldn't know that it was me who was calling. "Who's calling?"

"Santino, it's Serena," I said. "I'm in Mexico. I'm going to see Miguel."

He chuckled on the phone. "Miss Serena, it's good to hear from you. I'm in Italy. I need to lay low for a few days. I'll explain later. What can I do to help you out?"

"I need you to call Miguel," I said, "I'll be at his home in the next 10 hours or so," I said, "which means that I'll be there about five o'clock his time."

"Miss Serena, what are you doing? Where is Slade?"

"I have no clue. Are you going to call him?" I felt apprehensive, because if Santino didn't call this guy, there was no way I was going to be able to get in there and talk to this guy.

"What are you going to do when you get there?"

"I'm going to ask him about Charlotte. I have a recording device in my pocket, and then I'm..."

"Miss Serena, that sounds like a dumb idea, no offense. He has bodyguards who aren't going to let you get that recording device in there. You better put it in one of your body cavities."

That sounded gross, but also like it might work. It made me nervous, though, and I knew that I was going to have to go to a hospital to get it out. It was small enough to fit in either one of my "bodily cavities," yet, at the same time, it was large enough that a good surgeon could remove it if it got lost somewhere. It was also sensitive enough that it could record what was going on, even if I swallowed it. That why I bought this particular device. I somehow knew that I would one day need it. That day was now.

I felt nervous swallowing it, though. "Thanks for the advice," I said. "Listen, will this Miguel tell me what Charlotte did? And what is she doing, anyhow?" I couldn't believe that I never asked Santino this before - what leverage did Charlotte have over this guy?

Santino chuckled again. "Miguel has a daughter who wants to move to Hollywood and become a big star. Carlotta apparently has been promising him that she'll pull some strings. Get her an agent, put in a good word on her new movie, that kind of thing. Miguel hasn't jumped just yet, though, because Carlotta hasn't quite come through. As soon as she does, though, Miguel's going to be giving his big shipment to the Vichellis."

I shook my head. It was amazing to me that a big drug dealer would just tip from one family to another for something that was so trivial. Then again, helping his daughter in her career was probably important to him. The family is always important, and I got that. But in something as important as this…

"Really? That's all that she's promising?"

"Oh, no, I'm quite sure that she's used her womanly charms too. But, yeah, that's what she's promising. You have to understand, Serena, it's a toss-up between the two families. There won't be any downside for Miguel either way. Both families want this shipment badly, and both families want to do business with Miguel badly in the future. But if he chooses the Vichellis over the Garancinos, or the Garancinos over the Vichellis, the other family isn't going to come after him. So anything can tip him over, and that's what Carlotta is doing."

That made sense. I would imagine if Miguel had promised the Garancinos, then went back on his word, and gave the shipment to the Vichellis, there would be hell to pay. But, if he just hadn't made up his mind, then that was another matter.

I shook my head. Charlotte was a vindictive one, but I was surprised that she would do something against her own father like that. She had to know that it could bite her in the ass, as it hopefully was going to do. I wondered what kind of bad blood would have led her to do this.

Leverage. I was going to have leverage if this all worked

out right. Real leverage, assuming that her father would punish her for her disloyalty. I thought about the movie *The Godfather Part Two*, where Fredo was murdered at the behest of Michael, his own brother, and knew that, if there's a rat in the family, that rat will be taken care of. Daughter or not.

"Well, thanks, Santino. I really owe you a lot."

"No you don't, Miss Serena. After all, the reason why I'm on the street at all is because you worked that deal with the persecutor." Then he laughed. "Oh, I shouldn't call her a persecutor, because she got me a good deal. Guess I'll just call her a prosecutor."

I smiled, because Santino answered a burning question for me – whether or not he was using the term "persecutor" deliberately or because he didn't know any better. "Yes, they're not all bad after all, are they?"

"No, I guess not. Well, I'll give Miguel a call and let him know to expect you." He paused. "You be careful, Miss Serena. I don't think that you know what you're dealing with. Those are rough guys, and that's something coming from me. I think that you should be on the up and up on what you're doing. Tell him your situation, and tell him what you're going to do. Because if you do things without telling him, and it gets back to him, he'll kill you. You're a beautiful woman. Maybe he'll just go ahead and talk about that whole Carlotta thing with you. But you're probably going to have to do something for him first."

Do something for him first. What would that be? Sex, drug running, what? "What does that mean?"

"He'll probably want you to take a shipment over the border for him. That's usually what he asks for when people want favors. After all, if your plan goes through, his daughter is going to be the one who suffers. I hope that you realize that. I don't think that he's going to want to push his daughter under the bus like that."

Santino was making sense. If this whole thing played out the way that I wanted it to, Charlotte was going to be in serious trouble. She would obviously renege on her promise to Miguel to help Miguel's daughter, at the very least. I was going to have to give Miguel something in exchange for that. To make up for it. Because Santino was right – I couldn't just surreptitiously record him giving up Charlotte. Number one, he wasn't just going to give up Charlotte to me, a woman that he doesn't know from Eve. And number two, even if he did give up Charlotte, and I went behind his back to use it against him, he'd have me killed himself.

I'd be out of the frying pan and into the fire.

"Thanks for the advice," I said to Santino. "What do you recommend I give him in exchange for this information?"

"Miss Serena, you know Miguel's weakness. It's his daughter. If you could do something for his daughter, something that is equal to what Carlotta was doing, then you might be able to make a case. Other than that, I don't know. Probably he'll have you be a mule a time or two. He's always needing mules."

Egads. Being a mule would mean me putting drugs into my body cavities and trying to sneak it over the border. I took a deep breath, hoping that it wouldn't come to that, but knowing that if it did, I'd chance it. I'd chance anything for an opportunity to bring Charlotte down. Even if it meant that I was going to spend a few years in prison if I got caught.

That's how serious I was about bringing her down.

"Anything else he might want from me in exchange for this information?"

"Sex probably, but that would be in addition to your being a mule, not instead of it." He paused. "Miss Serena, I hate to say it, but it doesn't sound like you thought all this through."

"I didn't." I was embarrassed to admit how rashly I was acting. In the light of day, this whole thing seemed quixotic. Yet, in the light of day, I was still determined to go through with it. I would do anything, at that point, to see Charlotte hung up by her toes and batted with something hard. Or some other kind of torture. If there was anybody in the world who deserved it, it would be her.

I sighed, though. I would possibly be willing to be a mule. I wouldn't be willing to give him sexual favors. I wondered if he would be willing to deal with me on my terms.

Then I shook my head. My terms? I was going to be dictating the terms? What leverage did I have? I didn't have Hollywood connections. I....

I pulled over by the side of the road, realizing one thing – Slade was going to have to help me. I was being an idiot, an absolute idiot, for excluding him from this. He did have some leverage. He was loaded with money, but, more importantly, he had pharmaceutical connections. Miguel could probably use him and his connections. After all, many of the same ingredients that went into Oxytocin and other painkillers were the same ingredients as heroin. Miguel might be able to supply some stuff to Slade legally – opium, for instance. Slade might also be able to give Miguel a foothold in the legalized marijuana game in the states. Drug dealers were always looking for a way into that market, and Slade could maybe provide him with that.

One thing was for sure – Slade had things to offer that I just couldn't.

It was time to swallow my pride and give him a call. As much as I hated it, and as much as I currently hated him, I was going to have to use him.

I hung up with Santino, after we exchanged pleasantries, and dialed Slade's number.

I couldn't believe how nervous I was.

# Chapter Ten

## Slade

I boarded my private plane, after meeting Alex, and we were prepared for take-off, when my phone rang. My heart stopped as I looked at the number. The number didn't look familiar, but it looked like it was coming from another country. Hopefully Mexico.

Hopefully Serena.

"Hello?" I said, praying that I would hear Serena's voice on the other end of the line.

"Slade," Serena said, and I let out my breath. "I need you."

I felt like an enormous weight was taken off my shoulders. She called me, and said that she needed me. That was enough. I couldn't have felt more relieved. "Serena, where are you?"

"I'm on my way to a house here in Mexico. I probably shouldn't go into it too much over the phone, just in case…"

She didn't have to finish that sentence. Just in case Charlotte was somehow listening. "Serena, I need to know where you are. Where can I find you?"

"I'm still in Tijuana," she said. "I was going to leave this morning, but I talked to Santino, and, well, I need to tell you everything." She paused. "But Slade, I want you to know one thing. We're through, you and me. I saw that picture of you and Charlotte, and I know that you lied to me."

I sighed. "Serena, you should know better than that."

"Better than what? I saw what I saw."

"You didn't see what you see. I know what it looked like. But, trust me…"

"Don't say anything more. I'll see you at what time? I can get to the airport here and meet you if you want to bring your plane down."

"I won't say anything more right now, but I will when I see you. And I'm glad that you mentioned my bringing my plane." I smiled. She had perfect timing. I was going to go to Palermo, but I much preferred just flying down to Tijuana and getting Serena. I'd explain to her about that picture, because, I had to admit, it did look bad. "I'll meet you at the Tijuana airport, in the area where the private planes land. I'll get clearance right now to land."

"I'll see you soon."

I got off the phone and immediately let Alex know the change in plans. "We're not going to Palermo, but right on down to Tijuana. Get clearance and let's get out of here."

Alex nodded and got on the radio to get clearance and he nodded his head. "Tijuana, here we come."

It wasn't even an hour, more like 5 minutes, before I got to the Tijuana airport. Serena was able to find the area where we were to meet, and she was there. I went up to her and wrapped my arms around her. She stiffened up and put her hands on my chest, as if she were pushing me away. "Don't," she said, turning her face when I tried to kiss her. "I only called you because I need you to help me. I'm going to take Charlotte down, and I've realized that I need you to do that."

I drew a breath. "Serena, look at me," I said to her. I gently brought her face around so that she would be looking me in the eyes. "What you saw was more manipulation on Charlotte's part. I know about that picture. She set that up. She told the paparazzi to get a long-range photograph and to make it look like it was all spontaneous. She's a master of the game, I'll tell you that."

I saw in her eyes that she didn't really believe me, although her face did seem to soften just a little. She swallowed hard and then looked down at the ground.

"I don't understand. You mean that picture was staged?" She shook her head. "I mean, if it was a picture of the two of you in public, then, yeah, I'd totally believed it was staged. But it was behind closed doors. I…"

I stood there looking at her, knowing that she was turning my words around in her mind.

Then she drew a breath and hung her head. "God, I feel so stupid." When she looked at me, she had tears in her eyes. "So stupid. I was going to go on a suicide mission yesterday. An absolute suicide mission." Then she kind of laughed. "And the funny thing was, I didn't know exactly what the mission was going to be. I didn't plan a thing. I just went on autopilot, which is so unlike me. My life is so controlled all the time, and yesterday, well, it all went out the window. I finally cracked up, and it wasn't pretty."

I smiled at her. "It's okay to crack up, as long as you eventually come to your senses. And it sounds like you came to your senses before you did anything too rash and serious."

She smiled back. "Santino, of all people, managed to bring me back to reality. I was talking with him on the phone, and, as I spoke with him, I was realizing that my lack of planning wasn't going to do anything other than get me killed. If I didn't end up in a federal prison, because I was actually thinking of being a drug mule for a syndicate head down here. That's how far I was willing to go in order to bring down Charlotte. But Santino was making me realize what kind of dangerous game I was about to play, and how stupid I was being, so I called you. And I'm really glad that I did."

"I'm glad you did as well," I said, putting my hand in her hair. I put my hand on her chin and gave her a long kiss. She seemed to melt into me and I sighed. "Well, let's get this plane in the air. We can be at this place in…" It was then that I didn't know where I was going, or who I was seeing. "Where are we going?"

She smiled. "Ciudad Juarez. It's on the Texas border. It's about a ten hour drive, so probably we can be there in less than an hour. But Santino is calling Miguel, the guy that we're seeing, to give him a head's-up that I'm coming. The only thing is that Miguel won't be expecting me until late this evening."

"Okay, you're going to have to tell me who this Miguel is, and what he has to do with anything, and we can go from there."

"Miguel apparently is part of this enormous drug syndicate in Ciudad, and, well, he has a large shipment that he's going to give to one family – either the Garancinos or the Vichellis. He also is going to try to establish a relationship with one of the families, so that he can be the supplier going forward. And, believe it or not, Charlotte is in the middle of it. She's trying to tip Miguel over to the Vichellis."

The Vichellis? Why would she do that? Was I reading Charlotte wrong? I thought that she had a good relationship with her father. But that would explain why she was so weird when I asked her about meeting Gianni. "So Charlotte is double-crossing her own father?" That was fascinating to me in a weird way. It seemed so Shakespearean, really.

Yet, I had to get over my momentary fascination with the whole thing, to try to think more concretely. This was definitely something that I could use against Charlotte. More than that, it could be something that I could use to get the hit taken off of Serena permanently. Just the threat of telling Gianni what she was up to might be enough for her to permanently back off, and, if it wasn't, I could take what I know to Gianni and let the chips fall where they may. I knew about mob families – disloyalty can, and will, get you killed. It didn't even matter if you were close family – mob families rely on absolute trust within their ranks. Once that trust was gone, you were too.

"Okay, what is your plan on getting this information from Miguel? We're going to have to give proof to Gianni. We can't just go in there and tell Gianni what Charlotte is doing."

"I've had some time to think about that, which is why I need you." She lowered her head and cried. "Well, that's not true. I need you for other reasons. I need you to give me life and breath."

I let her cry for a few minutes before I gently prodded her to ask her exactly what she was thinking. I, too, needed her in my life. I knew how she felt. At the same time, though, there were pragmatic concerns. I needed to know what was going on in her head.

"Serena, let's talk about our plans."

She finally sighed and seemed to gather herself. "Okay, here's what I was thinking. We have to give Miguel something. According to Santino, Miguel is on the fence between these two families. Basically six of one, half-dozen of the other, and Charlotte is trying to put her thumb on the scales. That means that maybe we can give him something, too, to not only get Miguel to agree to go with Gianni, but also to give us the evidence that we're going to need to throw Charlotte under the bus for this."

I nodded my head, trying to process the information. "Okay, so, let's game this out. We give Miguel something, and we make him going to Gianni contingent on what we're going to give him. So then we have leverage with Gianni in a sense. Call off the hit for good in exchange for Miguel's business." That was sounding good. Really good. "Two birds, one stone. We throw Charlotte under the bus, while currying favor with Gianni. The only key is this – what do we give Miguel? What do we give him?"

I knew the answer to that. Money. Money always talked. The only thing was how much? And, also, how was I going to do business with a drug king-pin without getting in trouble myself? I was a legitimate businessman. If word ever got out about this, my shareholders would be spooked, to say the very least. I'd have to keep this extremely quiet, of course, but that was going to be tricky at best.

"Well, we could pay him a lot of money," she said, reading my mind. "But that might be risky. I was thinking of something else." She narrowed her eyes. "Where do you get your opiates for the drugs you manufacture?"

I nodded my head, knowing where she was going with this. "From Afghanistan. I buy them from legitimate suppliers over there. They're accredited and what they're doing is perfectly legal." I put my hand on my chin. "This Miguel person is not a legitimate supplier."

"No, but he has an opiate supply, ready and waiting to go." She raised an eyebrow and nodded her head, and I started to get the plan together in my head.

"My legitimate suppliers in Afghanistan get their opiates sometimes from the black market," I said, "it's like laundering, really. Everyone wins."

"Right. You get Miguel some contracts with some of your suppliers in Afghanistan...I'm sure that would be very valuable to him. And it'll be difficult to trace you back to him if you do it that way."

I drew a breath. "That could work. That could really work. I wonder if that would be enough incentive for him to go with the Garancinos, and I wonder if this deal that we propose would be enough for Miguel to threaten to withhold a contract with Gianni unless I come along with it."

Both of us sat in silence thinking this through. The downside, of course, is that Gianni himself could rat me out. But that was unlikely. He'd have no incentive to do so, and the downside for him would be immense – it would basically mean the loss of this suppliers contract with Miguel. ``

"Okay," said Serena. "We have an outline of how we should approach this. Let's try to get the specifics down." She smiled. "Who knew that Charlotte was enough of a bitch that she would try to throw her own father under the bus? Santino said that the reason why she hates him is because he apparently ordered the hit on Michael Garancino. She wants her revenge. Now we can use her thirst for vengeance against her. It's ironic, really."

The plane landed and we checked into a local hotel. We had to get all the specifics of our plan down, but, also, I had to admit that I wanted her badly. Needed to feel my skin on hers. Her skin was so soft, and just being close to her was getting my blood pumping.

But first thing first. We got into our hotel room, and sat down on one of the couches. The hotel wasn't grand, as there weren't a lot of choices in Ciudad, but it was clean and comfortable. Serena and I got out a notepad and started to scribble different numbers. I also got in contact with some of my suppliers in Afghanistan, and I found two who were willing to take shipment from Miguel. The shipments from Miguel to these suppliers would be worth in the neighborhood of $50 million to Miguel over the course of five years, so I knew that this would be enough for him to go back on his word to Charlotte.

At least I hoped that it would. Serena had explained to me that Miguel was working with Charlotte because he wanted his daughter to break into Hollywood.

"What if Miguel won't be swayed by money?" I asked Serena. "After all, the man probably had plenty of money. What if all he really wants is something intangible, like the chance for his daughter to make it in Hollywood?"

Serena and I had to cover all the bases, look at all the contingencies, so we would be more than ready for whatever Miguel decided to throw at us. Serena nodded her head. "I actually thought of that angle, too. Charlotte's contacts would be invaluable to Miguel's daughter, and if Charlotte took Miguel's daughter under her wing, that would really be something that could help the daughter. So, we have to perhaps sweeten the pot for Miguel. We have to give him some kind of reassurance that his daughter would still get her chance in Hollywood, even if he backs out of the deal with Charlotte."

"Well, then, okay," I said. "I do know Charlotte's publicist, and I also know quite a few movie producers and directors myself. I'll just tell Miguel that the daughter will be my project, and that I'll introduce her around to all the people I know. You forget that I've always run in the same circles as Charlotte. I know all the same people."

"You'll do that?"

"Of course. I mean, I'll have to do that if I tell him that I will. Granted, it won't be quite as effective as being seen as Charlotte's new BFF, if that is what Charlotte was promising him, but it'll be the next best thing. Our combining this offer with the offer to give him a long-term buyer in Afghanistan might be powerful enough for him to jump."

Serena took a deep breath. "Yes, but he not only has to jump, but he has to be willing to go on the record on what Charlotte was doing. That's pretty important. If he won't go on the record, then we have no evidence, and we're right back where we started. Which is nowhere, really."

I drew a breath. "And we'll actually make this much worse, really, if we can't get him on the record. Because it's going to piss off Charlotte, and her father still won't know what she was up to. So, we're gambling here, really, because we have no idea what this guy is going to do. Plus, the mere fact that I'm down here with you is going to piss off Charlotte, too. I'm not naïve enough to think that Charlotte has no clue on where I am right now."

"That means that we need to get to Miguel as soon as possible. After all, she might beat us down there."

I knew that Serena was right. But I wasn't entirely sure if Charlotte had a way to track me. I was smart enough to get a completely new phone before coming down here, and I regularly had my plane and car swept for bugs. Nothing had yet turned up. If Charlotte did track me, she would had to have been much more savvy than I gave her credit for.

Serena did make a point, though. There really wasn't a second to waste. Miguel was expecting us by this 8 in the evening, according to what Serena had told me about Santino. It was presently seven, so we were chomping at the bit to get to the compound.

We took a deep breath, and held hands on the way to Serena's car.

Here goes nothing.

# Chapter Eleven

## Serena

To say that my heart was pounding as Slade and I sat in my car, going to see Santino, would be a serious, serious understatement. I had no clue on how this whole mission was going to go. I could only go on what Santino told me about this guy, and Slade was absolutely right. If this whole plan went to hell, we would not only not succeed, but we would be making things worse. Charlotte would be furious, and I would imagine that she would double-down on her threats and would probably renege on the whole Slade deal. Slade was demonstrating his disloyalty to her, and she would never again be able to trust him.

The upshot is that, if this whole thing went south, I probably wouldn't have long to live. Nor Slade. The stakes couldn't possibly be higher.

Oh, but if it worked…it would possibly mean that Slade and I could be together. Charlotte would no longer have the backing of her father, which would mean that the Garancinos wouldn't be after me. Charlotte still would be, but she was only one woman. I could handle her. Slade could handle her as well. She was psychotic, but it would simply be a matter of hiring a decent bodyguard to protect both of us, and all would probably be okay.

But if the Garancinos were involved, especially her father...no bodyguard in the world would be able to protect us from that. The Garancinos were ruthless and lethal, not to mention cunning. They dispatched with their enemies with ease.

Neutralizing the father, therefore, was the only way to handle this situation. And that wasn't going to be easy, even if Slade and I could convince Miguel to turn. Even if Slade and I got Miguel on the record on what Charlotte was doing. There still would be a gamble that Gianni would still show loyalty to his daughter over us, and that would mean that the whole plan would still backfire.

As intricate as this whole situation was, not to mention dangerous, I knew that it would still be better than the status quo – no matter the outcome. At least we were doing something to fight back. That was the main thing.

I reached my hand over to Slade. "I'm surprised that Charlotte hasn't tried to call you."

Slade shook his head. "Serena, you know me. I'm surprised that you wouldn't have figured out that I got an entire new phone before I came down here. New number and everything. I could never trust that the whole phone didn't have some kind of a bug in it, so I ditched it."

That was a good thing, but, at the same time, it was a bad thing, too. Charlotte had no way of getting ahold of Slade, and she was probably going out of her ever-loving mind. That could possibly make her even more dangerous. But Slade was smart, too, for doing that – God forbid Charlotte would track us down here. She'd be waiting for us at Miguel's compound for sure if that were the case.

Slade looked at me. "Are you thinking what I'm thinking?"

"Of course. Everything has to break our way, and I mean everything. One little thing happens that goes wrong, and all bets are off. The most that we can hope for is to convince Miguel not to tell Charlotte that we were down here, if this plan doesn't go through. I suppose that could work if Charlotte has no way of tracking you."

Slade nodded his head. "You make a point. If Miguel won't jump, and we say no harm, no foul, I suppose I could pay him to keep quiet about us paying him a visit. That might be the only way yet to save our necks here."

I had to smile. Could our necks be saved at all?

I decided to make some small talk to take our minds off the situation at hand. "You know, Derek was fired. Thanks for doing that."

Slade reached his hand and it covered my own. "That was the first thing that I did, of course. I didn't want you to be subjected to that asshole for one more day. Charlotte was okay with me doing that, because, after all, she got what she wanted, which was me. That's all that really mattered to her. She was just fine with Derek getting gone, because he ceased to be useful to her. That's how Charlotte is – she uses people and then discards them when they no longer serve her purpose. She's such a crazy, crazy bitch."

"You think?"

"Oh, yeah. I think."

We finally ended up on the edge of the compound. Standing by the edge of the gate were two men in army fatigues and black berets on their head. They both were over six feet tall, and built like brick shit-houses. They carried high-powered AR-15s, and they both looked at us suspiciously.

One of the men came up to the car and spoke in rapid Spanish. I looked over at Slade, not understanding a word.

Slade, however, nodded his head and spoke back in rapid Spanish. The conversation didn't seem at all heated, though, so I held my breath and said a little prayer. I closed my eyes and tried to tune into the vibrations of the man with the gun, and I felt that he wasn't angry or suspicious. He simply was asking questions, a lot of them, and I knew why. He obviously didn't let just anyone in through these gates. If he did, I would imagine that his boss, Miguel, would soon be dead.

I heard the name "Santino," come out of Slade's mouth. I was amused that Santino's name was spoken with a Spanish accent, as Slade's accent seemed to be spot-on. He grasped my hand and looked at me briefly. I could tell, by his expression, that things were going to be okay, at least for the time being.

Finally, after what seemed like forever, the guy in the beret let us go on through the gates. Slade waved at the guy, and the guy waved back in a friendly gesture. "Gracias," Slade said, the one word that I knew.

"De nada," the guy said with a smile. Then he said, in broken English, "Good luck."

As we drove on the dirt road that led to the compound, I turned to Slade. "What was that all about?"

Slade shrugged. "Nothing. He was just questioning me on why I was there. I told him that Santino had sent us, and that seemed to change everything. From there, we just talked about what I planned to say to Miguel, and I just said that I was going to try to negotiate a business deal. I didn't explain to him the details, of course. I don't think that he really wanted details. Going through him was really just a formality. After he heard the name 'Santino,' he was ready to let us go on through."

I guessed that Santino had quite a relationship with this Miguel person. I didn't know that Santino was so trusted, but I was certainly happy that he was. Of course.

"Okay," Slade said to me. "Well, we're through the first phase of this. We're through the gates, and we're heading to the main house. Chico, the man that I just spoke to, just radioed ahead to Miguel that we're going to meet with him, so he's going to be expecting us." Slade swallowed hard. "It's now or never. Gut-check time. Either we get what we want, or…"

I nodded my head. "Or we don't, and we just made things worse. After all, even if Miguel agrees to keep quiet about this whole thing, that doesn't get us out of the woods. Charlotte is going to be wondering where you are, and you know that she's going to highly suspect that you're with me. She's going to go through the roof."

"Well, we gotta go in there with confidence and swagger," Slade said, and I smiled. Confidence and swagger were definitely two qualities that came naturally to him. "Make the case, and then see what happens."

"Yeah," I said, "if he doesn't kill us first." Who knows? Maybe he was so loyal to Charlotte that he would give us both bullets in the head as soon as we got in the door. Slade and I were certainly flying blind, in a way.

We finally got up the house, after following a dirt road for what seemed like miles, and the dirt road turned into a paved one that led smoothly into a circle drive. I marveled at how "ordinary" Miguel's house seemed. Not ordinary in that it wasn't opulent, because it certainly was. It was Spanish-style, and enormous. Large windows that curved elegantly. Spanish tiles on the roof. It was stucco, and seemed to be at least three stories tall. The door was enormous and heavy, and there was a bird that was carved into it. In the middle of the circle drive was an enormous fountain that had a statue of two little children, with water jugs, and these water jugs were what appeared to be pouring out the water for the fountain.

In all, this house seemed like it would be owned by a wealthy patron of the arts, maybe, or perhaps a movie director who had unusually elegant taste. I guess I shouldn't have been surprised, but I was. After all, this mansion was owned by a drug King-pin. I imagined, before we got to the house, that it would be something that was gaudy. Enormous, but not with tasteful architecture and appointments.

When the door opened, after we knocked, and a small and rotund lady in a maid's uniform opened it, I was further amazed by how the house was laid out inside. It looked, for all the world, like an art museum. The top ceiling was a good fifty feet above the floor where we stood, and it was an open-air design. On the top of the ceiling was a mural that looked like it was a stellar replica of a famous Renaissance painting, or a series of Renaissance paintings. Angels, devils, gods and mortals all convened above our heads in perfect detail. The floor beneath us was a tan marble, with patterns running throughout.

While the ceiling was fifty feet above our heads, there also were, to the side, floors that surrounded us on the side. It was like the center of this first room was an atrium, and the floors were on the sides of it. Like a hotel. In the center of the foyer, or whatever this first room was, was another huge fountain, surrounded by couches, tables and chairs, which were tastefully and strategically placed. On the walls were more paintings – some looked like they were Chinese, as they featured Chinese houses, mountains and people. Others looked Renaissance. Still others looked modern. Despite the fact that the art work in this room was diverse, everything seemed to flow together seamlessly. Nothing seemed to clash, but, because everything was strategically placed, it all came together beautifully.

And, everywhere we looked, there were crucifixes. They were both in the paintings that we saw, and on the walls. Yet, they didn't look like they were out of place. Like everything else, they blended in beautifully with the décor.

In all, I had to admit, I admired this guy's aesthetic. He might have been a ruthless drug dealer, but he certainly seemed to have a soft, feminine side to him. The beauty and tranquility that surrounded us in that house told me that Miguel was somebody who prided himself on his image and had a cultured aesthetic.

I wondered if all that could be used. Maybe he would be somewhat reasonable, after all. I tried not to get sucked into what the vision of the house might mean, but my mind was turning over the possibilities. He cared about image, he cared about beauty, and his mind seemed to be much more subtle than I had given him credit for.

I cleared my throat and looked over at Slade. "This place is like a museum," I whispered to him. "Literally."

Slade nodded. "It certainly is. I'm not surprised, but, at the same time, I kinda am. After all, he's not married. At least I don't think that he is, from what you've told me. He does have a daughter, though. The daughter is sixteen, so I doubt that she hired an interior decorator to design this place."

I suddenly knew that, along with the offers we were going to give Miguel, that we should sweeten the pot with one more thing – flattery. Since this guy obviously had taken such pride to make sure that this house looked just how he wanted it, even going so far as to apparently appoint a decorator and art curator for the job, he could probably be swayed by some smooth talk.

It made sense, really. After all, this was a man who had enough of a sensitive side that he was swayed by offers to help his daughter. That was the deal-maker, apparently. That meant that this Miguel wasn't your typical thug. This was confirmed by looking at this house.

I suddenly felt more calm about meeting this guy. I couldn't put my finger on it, but I felt that Slade and I just might have a chance. I looked over at him and then closed my eyes. I felt that he looked calm, and he felt calm as well.

I hoped that we weren't having false hopes.

Finally, after what seemed like hours, but probably was only minutes, a woman came to see us. "Ola," she said, and then proceeded to speak in perfect English. There was a slight accent, but, other than that, she seemed to be extremely fluent. "Mr. Sanchez will see you now." She nodded her head slightly and motioned for us to follow her.

I took an enormous breath and got up from my seat. I held Slade's hand as we followed this woman. She looked back at us and smiled. She was really quite beautiful – black hair, hazel eyes, slight frame and her smile lit up the room. I had no idea who she was, but she was trying to make us both feel comfortable, so that was another good sign.

It seemed like we went through an enormous maze, but, finally, we were directed to a room. It was an ornate room, classically designed like the rest of the house. Red carpet, dark wood paneling, but the ceiling was a good twenty feet high and decorated with a Renaissance style mural. A small man was sitting behind a large desk. He seemed to be forty-ish, dark-skinned, with a large nose and pock marks on his face. He was dressed in a three-piece suit, as if he was waiting for some high-powered attorney to meet him. In his pocket was a little handkerchief that was multi-colored. And, like with the rest of the house, this room also had a crucifix.

He smiled broadly as we walked through the door. He extended his hand, and Slade and I shook it. He offered his hand to Slade first, which told me that he probably was more interested in doing business with Slade then with me. This was in keeping with the paternalistic nature of the country, I knew, and Miguel struck me as also being paternalistic. I just got that vibe from him.

"Hello," he said, "You must be Slade and Serena." He nodded. "I understand that you wanted to talk to me about a business agreement."

I took a deep breath and looked over at Slade. He looked at ease as Miguel motioned for the two of us to sit down in the chairs that are in front of the desk. Slade sat down, and I did as well, although I felt slightly uneasy. I certainly felt more uneasy than Slade seemed to be. As I closed my eyes, though, and tuned into Slade's vibrations, I felt that his outward calm was simply a façade. Internally, he was churning.

"Yes," Slade said to Miguel. "I hope you don't mind if I get down to business. I know that you're a busy man, so I want to take as little of your time as possible."

Miguel nodded his head. "I am a busy man, as are you. I understand that you are the CEO of Bridgewell Industries. Very impressive."

"I am," Slade said. "You've done your homework."

"I have. As I'm sure you have done the same with me."

Slade nodded his head. I was sure that Miguel knew more about Slade then Slade knew about him, though. I studied Miguel and I realized that he probably knew quite a bit about Slade. Perhaps it was because he did his home-work on Slade, or maybe it was just because of Slade's noto-riety with the murder case. Or maybe it was because Slade had always been something of a minor celebrity, mainly because he was a handsome billionaire who routinely squired actresses and super-models. Maybe it was combina-tion of these factors.

"Yes," Slade said. "I have."

I admired the way that Slade was able to act so comfort-able and relaxed, even though I knew that he really wasn't inside. I supposed that this façade of his came in handy when he was trying to negotiate his business deals, because a poker face goes a long way towards getting what you want in the business world.

The two men studied one another for a few minutes, and then Miguel finally spoke. "Can I get you something to drink? Cristal, scotch, rum, vodka?"

"I'd like a Dewar's neat, thank you."

Miguel looked at me. "I'd like the same," I said. I didn't like to drink while I was trying to negotiate deals myself, but when in Rome...

Miguel poured us both a neat scotch, and I took a sip. It was smooth and high-dollar, which relieved me. I didn't enjoy drinking straight liquor usually, but this was tasty.

We all had our liquor and Slade was carefully sipping his. He needed to have a clear mind for what was at hand, so I knew that was why he was nursing his drink.

Slade finally cleared his throat. "Mr. Sanchez, I'd like to make a proposal to you. I understand that you have a ship-ment of some high-grade heroin and cocaine that you would like to provide to one of two families – either the Vichellis or the Garancinos."

Miguel narrowed his eyes. I knew why – he was sizing up Slade, trying to determine if Slade was on the up and up. For all Miguel knew, this whole thing could be just a trap for him. Granted, Santino set this whole meeting up, and I presumed that Santino was trusted by Miguel. But Miguel could never be too careful, I knew, as somebody in his position can never quite be sure that somebody isn't going to double-cross him.

He finally nodded his head imperceptibly. "Yes, that is true." He looked up at the ceiling, and I knew that there was something up there. Probably a person who would swoop down and gun down Slade and me if there was any kind of a hint that something was amiss.

Slade stood up, his arms crossed in front of him. He paced a little and put his hand on his chin. "Mr. Sanchez, I happen to know that you are getting ready to give your shipment to the Vichellis. I understand that Carlotta Garancino has been negotiating with you in an attempt to persuade you to go with the Vichellis over the Garancinos."

Miguel again narrowed his eyes. "Yes, that is true. She has offered me something that money cannot buy. So, if you are here to try to persuade me to change my mind, I have to tell you that you are wasting your time."

At that, he looked up in the same area of the ceiling, and I started to feel uneasy. Were we about to be ambushed?

"I know what Carlotta has offered you, and I'm here to offer you something that can replace that, plus something more. Value-added, you might say."

Miguel nodded. "Value-added. That sounds interesting. I'll give you a hearing. Since you know what it is that Ms. Garancino has offered me, then I would imagine that your substitution will be just as effective. So, please, proceed Mr. Bridgewell."

"I understand that you have a young daughter who would like to break into Hollywood. Carlotta has promised you that, if you give your shipment to the Vichellis, she will help your daughter get a foothold in the movie industry. Mr. Sanchez, I do not think that you know much about Carlotta."

I thought it was a bit odd that Slade kept calling Charlotte "Carlotta," instead of referring to her as "Ms. Garancino," as Miguel was doing, but I figured that there was a reason for doing so.

"Yes," Miguel said, taking a sip of his drink. "You are correct. My daughter's name is Mandolina, and, as you note, she is a young girl. Only 16 years old." He got out his wallet and showed us a picture of the girl. She was gorgeous and curvaceous, with olive skin, dark eyes, black hair and delicate features. She had a beautiful smile, with straight teeth, full lips and high cheekbones. I had no idea how tall she was, but if she was at least 5'9", she could make it in the modeling world without a problem. The camera absolutely loved her. She was incandescent.

Slade studied the picture and looked at Miguel. "I can see from this picture that she has the physical profile that will take her far in Hollywood. I do not know her background, however. What sort of acting work has she done? What is she interested in?"

"She's interested in both modeling and acting. As you can see, she is very beautiful." He drew a breath and looked down at his glass. "As was her mother."

He looked at his glass for a long time after he said that last line, and I could tell, even without trying to tune into his vibrations, that the issue of Mandolina's mother was a sore subject for him.

I tentatively decided to join the conversation. "Mandolina's mother. Where is she?" It really was none of my business, but I was looking for any kind of an opening. That was always the secret to negotiations, in my view – trying to find common ground. Make the person really like you. True, I also got what I wanted through some ball-busting, but I always preferred to attract the bees with honey instead of vinegar.

Miguel again took a deep breath, and looked at the ceiling. He spoke softly in Spanish, and I studied Slade. I knew that Slade knew what Miguel was saying, so I was going to have to ask him later. Miguel swallowed hard, his Adam's Apple prominently bobbing up and down. He finally looked at both of us, his face composed.

"So," he said, addressing Slade. "Why do you ask about my daughter? As you know, Ms. Garancino has a huge advantage in the movie world just now. Nobody hotter on the scene than her. What can you offer me that would match that?"

I studied Miguel, wondering why he deliberately ignored my question. I know that he heard me. Why did he pretend that I never spoke at all?

Slade cleared his throat and looked over at me. There was something in his demeanor that had changed. I couldn't put a finger on it, but I just had a feeling. He took a deep breath, and took a sip of his scotch. Then he raised an eyebrow and looked at me again.

"I can offer you a supplier's contract. Long-term. I have a supplier in Afghanistan. That's where I get my opioids for the medicines that I produce. I've talked to my Afghan supplier, and they would be willing to enter into a three-year contract with you for all the opioids that you can supply. So, it would be open-ended, and worth millions to you. You'll have an option, of course, at the end of the three-year contract to extend it if your working relationship is satisfactory. I think that this would be an excellent opportunity for you to really break into a lucrative region of the world."

Miguel narrowed his eyes. "That is it?" Then he shook his head. "Mr. Bridgewell, look around. I have enormous wealth. I do not need additional contracts, although I thank you very much for your offer. It is very generous, do not get me wrong. But what Carlotta has offered me is more precious to me than any multi-million dollar contract. I can get those anywhere. What I cannot get anywhere is a chance for my daughter to realize her dream. Carlotta has offered me this."

Slade looked over at me, and I knew. I knew that Slade had a feeling that Miguel was going to turn down this offer. That was why he had such an odd look on his face before. There was something in what Miguel was saying in Spanish that made Slade realize that this Afghan thing was never going to fly.

I cleared my throat. "Mr. Sanchez," I said, trying one more time. Something told me that the issue of Mandolina's mother would be the key to it all. "I'm really so sorry to ask this, but what happened to Mandolina's mother? You said-" I was about to bring up the fact that Miguel had referred to the mother in past tense, but Miguel cut me off.

"Mr. Bridgewell, do you have any other offer for me? Because, I am very sorry. As you noted before, I am a very busy man."

Slade opened his mouth and then shook his head. "No." He looked over at me. "Serena, I think that it's time that we leave Mr. Sanchez." He stood up and offered his hand to me. Then he shook Miguel's hand. "Mr. Sanchez, it was a pleasure to meet you. I am very sorry that we cannot do business."

I furrowed my brow at Slade, and he furtively glanced at me. His expression told me all that I needed to know. *Just trust me,* his expression said. *I got this.*

I shook my head. Charlotte was going to be missing Slade soon and would be putting an APB out on him. If she somehow figured out what was going on here on this compound, she would be livid and who knows? She might show up and accelerate the deal. Once the deal was sealed, that would be it. Our window would be closed.

Our window would be closed and our goose would be cooked. She'd have us both dead by the time the sun came up. Miguel would rat on us, tell her what we just tried, and that would be it.

With a beating heart, I took Miguel's out-stretched hand. "It was a pleasure," I said, as Miguel kissed it.

"The pleasure was mine." His smile was soft, and his eyes seemed kind.

He pressed a button, and the same woman who led us back to Miguel's study or office of whatever this magnificent room was, appeared and led us back through the house.

When we got back out, into the sunlight, I glanced at Slade.

"Don't ask right now," he said. "I have a plan, and we have to execute it soon. And I mean soon."

I nodded my head as we got into my car and drove off. I was dying to find out what Slade knew, but it was just going to have to wait.

# Chapter Twelve

We drove off, and Slade took my hand. "Okay, here's the deal. Mandolina's mother isn't dead. That much I got."

"Okay. How do you know?"

"He doesn't know that I know Spanish fluently. He was speaking rapidly, but I understood every word. Remember that? He looked up at the ceiling and spoke aloud?"

"Yes, of course. That was why I was trying to ask him what happened to the mother. I hated to pry like that, but I somehow knew that the mother was going to be the key to this whole thing."

"It is. He said her name. It's Marguerita. He was saying, in Spanish, that he would give up all of his wealth if he could have one more year with her. She wasn't around, of course, but it would be fairly easy to figure out where she is. I just have to talk to my computer hacker, Ivan, to get the records on where she is. He might even be able to figure out what's wrong with her. It's a long shot, but, hey, I'm a drug developer. What if I could offer Miguel a cure for whatever is wrong with her?"

"Slade, isn't that asking too much? I mean, we have to figure something out, and figure it out quickly. Once Charlotte finds out what we're doing, we're both literally dead. Literally. What if she has terminal cancer or something? You know that you don't have a drug for everything."

Slade reached out his hand. "Listen, let's just find out what is wrong with Marguerita, and then I can maybe figure it out. You forget that my company has developed numerous drugs that aren't on the market yet, because they're still going through clinical trials and have yet to be approved. I have some very promising drugs that have been shown to combat many different kinds of cancer, drugs that aren't available to the general public. What if I could help Marguerita with something like that? Give Miguel something that isn't available to the public yet, but has promise? Might he go for a Hail Mary like that? Would it be worth it to him?"

I shook my head. "That sounds dangerous. And, besides, you couldn't cure your mother's pancreatic cancer. I mean, when you thought that she had pancreatic cancer. You never suggested giving her something off-market."

"That's because I haven't yet found an effective treatment for that particular kind of cancer. Nobody has. Everybody's trying, of course, but, since it's rather rare, compared to other types of cancer, there hasn't been that much money in finding something." He shook his head. "Listen, it's worth a shot, isn't it? If he's going to be swayed by Charlotte helping his daughter, he might really be swayed by a chance to help his wife."

I nodded my head. "Why didn't you go with our original plan of helping his daughter in our own way? You know, because you know the same people and all of that."

Slade shook his head. "I made a snap decision not to. It

just hit me that Charlotte could really help his daughter, because Charlotte is so in demand right now. I know that I don't have the same connections or the same cache as Charlotte does in the movie business. I literally made a quick decision not to go down that road. I don't think that it would have worked, and, even if Miguel made the decision for me to help Mandolina, instead of Charlotte, I feel that I wouldn't do Mandolina justice."

"Sometimes it happens like that, I guess. You go into a negotiation, and read the room, so to speak, and immediately decide against using a pre-planned strategy. That's happened to me more times than I can count."

Of course, my being an empath was part of the reason why I often changed course in the middle of a negotiation. I could always get a vibration on what would work and what wouldn't, and that usually made me change my mind and try something different. That made me a very successful negotiator.

What impressed me is that Slade had that same skill. He was able to read Miguel and immediately decide to change strategy. Of course, we still weren't entirely clear on exactly what that strategy entailed. I only knew that it was going to have something to do with possibly finding a cure of the ailing Marguerita.

Slade turned into our hotel. "Okay, I'm going to call Ivan. I have to find out where Marguerita is, and, hopefully, get her records. Once I find out what we're dealing with, I can hopefully figure out a plan to get Miguel on our side."

At that, we went into the lobby and took the elevator to our suite. When we got into our suite, Slade called Ivan. "Ivan," Slade said, "I need you to find some information out for me.....Marguerita Sanchez, address------....yes, I need to know where she is staying right now...find out what her medical condition is as well if you can...thank you."

Slade got off the phone and sat down on the chair. "Well, now, we wait. We wait and find out what is going on with Marguerita. After we find that out, we find out how to approach Miguel."

I smiled. "You know, I knew when I saw his house that there was more to the story. I would imagine that his wife was the one who decorated it, or had it decorated. It was just too perfect, too feminine. Not that this man doesn't have a feminine side, because I imagine he does. But seeing that house...." I shook my head. "I just kinda knew that there was something to it."

"I did too. It's pretty obvious that we're dealing with somebody who loves something more than money. I can't believe that I offered him a contract worth millions and he turned that down flat." He brought me down on his lap and nuzzled my neck. "Turns out that even wealthy drug king-pins can have a heart. And pharmaceutical CEOs."

I sighed, wanting and needing to feel him inside of me. I turned my head to him and he kissed me lightly. I closed my eyes as his kisses started to become more urgent. "I missed you," I whispered. "Like you wouldn't believe."

"Oh, I believe," he said. "I felt the same. There wasn't any way that I would have been able to stay away from you for any length of time." He kissed me more passionately and I could feel his hard-on through his pants.

He carried me to the bed, and he lay beside me, stroking my hair. I closed my eyes, wanting to revel in his touch. I wanted to drink it in, just in case I never saw him again. That was possible, after all. If Charlotte beat us to Miguel, then that would be it. Game over.

He put his hand on my cheek and kissed me slowly. I

sighed as he slowly and gently stripped off my clothes. I craved less vanilla, but, for now, vanilla would do. Vanilla was heavenly. Vanilla was exactly what I needed.

He stripped off his clothes too, and entered me languidly. He was going to make this last, and I wanted him to. I needed him to. As he rocked in and out, I came to orgasm after orgasm.

———————

Later on that night, after we made love several times, I just lay next to him and watched him while he slept. He woke with a start and his eyes locked with mine. "What's going on?" he asked me.

I shrugged. "I'm just nervous." I drew a deep breath. "This might be..."

"Stop. We're going to get through this. We're going to get through this."

He spread his arms and I lay in them. For now, just for now, I felt safe.

## Chapter Thirteen

The next day, Ivan called Slade. "What did you find out?" Slade asked.

I watched as he wrote down the words "Huntington's Disease." He nodded slowly and screwed up his face. He then put his head in his hands. "Thank you," he told Ivan. "Thanks for the information."

I knew something about that disease. It was degenerative and almost always fatal, if not 100% fatal. I had no idea if Slade had something in the pipeline that would help.

He took a deep breath. "Huntington's Disease. We don't have a cure for that."

I knew that. "Right. But I've heard of..."

"Promising therapies, including genetic editing? Yes, that's probably the most promising therapy out there today. My company has been working on actually doing just that, along with a lot of other companies. But..." He shook his head. "What can I bring to the table that other companies cannot? I need to have something, otherwise I just violated a woman's privacy for no reason. That will just make things that much worse."

"Slade, this might help. I don't know. But what if you promise to work on finding a cure for this disease? You said that your company has been using this genetic editing idea, and that it's promising. What if you make a commitment to this disease, and you can present that to Miguel? It'll give him some hope at least."

Slade gave me a look that I couldn't quite discern. "I don't know about this. My company is on the forefront, really, of this particular therapy. But it doesn't feel right. I'll be committing to finding a cure for this in exchange for a massive drug shipment going to one mob family. That's not why I wanted to go into pharmaceuticals. I want to find cures for rare diseases, of course, and all diseases really. But agreeing to pursue a course of action in exchange for a drug shipment sounds..."

"Unethical. I know. But look at it this way – there are people all over the world suffering from this disease. They'll all be helped immensely if you do this. If you find a cure, you'll be helping so many people. It'll be something wonderful that came out of this entire mess if you really think about it."

Slade nodded his head. "Okay. So, I make a commitment to pour let's say $50 million into finding a cure for Huntington's. Miguel's no fool, though. He's going to want to make sure that I'm as good as my word. I could give him a list of researchers who I have working on this, and their credentials. I could also give him a copy of all the clinical trials that our company already has underway, as well as all the trials that we're conducting in the future. I don't really know what else I can give him except my word."

"He might take it," I said. "After all, just the possibility that you'll be working feverishly on finding a cure for this disease might be enough to sway him. It's better than anything that he has now. He'll have a personal company who can keep him in the loop on all the breakthroughs, and he'll be guaranteed that Margeurita can get into a clinical trial as soon as the therapy becomes promising. As it is now, Margeurita may or may not be able to take part in a clinical trial, and he probably doesn't have anybody that he can just pick up the phone and call about progress. Tell him that you'll be that guy. The guy that he can talk to whenever. That's probably what he wants and needs."

Slade nodded his head. "Okay, then, it's worth a shot. It's really the only shot we have."

I tilted my head. "Where is Marguerita?"

"She's at the house, of course. She has nurses with her around the clock. She's apparently been symptomatic for two years. At the very least, I can offer him the drugs that my company has already developed to treat the symptoms of Huntington's now. There are quite a few that I can offer, including some that are not yet available to the general public but will be within the next few months."

"That sounds promising, really. You can offer him some new drugs for her months in advance. That would be price-less, because that represents a few months that she doesn't have to suffer as much because she'll be getting all the latest drugs even before they come onto the market."

We made our way out of the hotel and into my car. "Well, here goes nothing. He's either going to kill us because we invaded his wife's privacy or he's going to give us anything we ask for. Let's hope it's the latter, of course."

As we drove along the highway on the way to Miguel's, I said a silent prayer.

It was now or never, of course.

## Chapter Fourteen

We arrived at Miguel's at just after 10 AM. He wasn't expecting us, as Slade wanted to surprise him. The reasoning for this was because this was a negotiation that could only be done in person, and he couldn't really explain to Miguel over the phone why he wanted to come back to see him. The upshot was that there was a chance, probably a big chance, that Miguel was going to send both of us on our way.

That is if we didn't face Charlotte in the house. That was also a risk.

As we got to the gates of the estate, we were greeted with the same two men in berets. Slade simply smiled. "Hello, we were here yesterday. We'd like to see Miguel again today."

One of the men looked at Slade and me suspiciously. "Why are you going to see him today? I do not think that you have an appointment."

"We don't. But I wanted to see him. I'm a pharmaceutical CEO, as he knows, and I'd like to negotiate with him about possibly finding a cure for his wife." No use beating around the bush. Miguel was either going to be pissed beyond belief or he was going to let us in to see him. That would have been the outcome either way, so at least we knew what to expect at the outset.

Beret man grimaced and then spoke in rapid Spanish into his two-way radio. Rapid Spanish speaking came right back, and, to my relief, Beret man nodded at us and waved us through.

I let out a huge breath. This was a good sign. He was going to listen to us. He was going to hear us out. I looked over at Slade as we drove along. "What did Miguel say in Spanish?"

"Nothing, really. He just said to let us in. That doesn't mean that he actually wants to talk with us. It might mean that he wants to kill us." Slade smiled slyly, but I didn't. He might have been joking – I think – but I found nothing funny about this situation. Whatsoever.

We drove along the dirt road, and, to my surprise, Miguel was waiting for us outside. He was sitting at a small table that in front of the house, smoking a cigar and squinting in the sun at us. Slade and I gave each other a look. Both of us were apprehensive. I knew this. My stress was through the roof, and Slade's was palpable. I didn't even have to tune into his vibrations to know this.

I tried to get a read on Miguel, but I couldn't. There was something that was blocking me, so I had no idea what was going through his mind as he stared at the two of us.

We got out of the car. I knew that I was walking with trepidation, but Slade confidently strode towards Miguel. Slade had a smile on his face, and I once again marveled at how well he was able to cover up what he was actually feeling. "Hello again, Mr. Sanchez," Slade said. "Thank you for agreeing to meet with us again."

Miguel regarded Slade with deep suspicion, yet motioned to a chair. "Sit down Mr. Bridgewell," Miguel said. "Let's talk."

Slade looked over at me and I nervously sat in another chair that Miguel had motioned to. I clasped my hands in front of me on the table and tried to stay quiet. Slade held all the cards in this, so I was going to let him do the negotiations.

Miguel began the conversation. "You know about my wife," he said. And then he nodded. "I am impressed. It certainly did not take you long to find out about her condition."

I let out a small sigh of relief. It seemed that Miguel wasn't angry with us for invading his wife's privacy after all.

Slade nodded his head. "I do. I'm very sorry to hear about her condition. I know that it's difficult for you."

Miguel didn't say anything for a long time. He stared at the horizon, and didn't move a muscle. Slade and I were sitting at the little table, silently. We both knew that Miguel was going to talk to us soon about what was going on. It was just a matter of time.

He finally spoke. "Marguerita's mother had the condition. For years. Couldn't move or think by the end. Degenerated slowly but surely. Couldn't swallow, so had to eat through a tube. Couldn't stop...twitching. Jerking. Then her muscles would completely freeze. Those were the first signs. Then she couldn't speak. Wouldn't remember simple words. Forgot Marguerita's name. Wouldn't want to leave the house, and was in bed all the time. After about a year of that, Anita, my Marguerita's mother, saw a doctor. Did tests for a year before being diagnosed with this horrible disease."

He shook his head. "The seizures. The constant threat of suicide. The slow decline. It took its toll on everyone. Then she couldn't move at all, had to get the feeding tube, did not recognize anyone." He took a deep breath. "When Marguerita got her diagnosis, just last week, we agreed that we would have one year together. One good year, and then..."

I knew what was going to happen at the end of that year without Miguel even telling me. I knew that Marguerita and Miguel had agreed that she would have one year with him, and then she would commit suicide. Those words were unspoken, but they were written on his face. I felt for this man immensely.

"Where is Marguerita now?" I asked softly.

He shrugged. "She's in her bedroom," he said haltingly and softly. "She has good days and bad days. Mainly bad. It seems that things are progressing much faster than with her mother. I don't know..." He pinched the bridge of his nose as he evidently tried to hold back tears. "I hope that we can have our year."

Slade cleared his throat. "Mr. Sanchez, I think that I can help you. I cannot guarantee anything, though, except you have my word that I will commit tremendous resources to finding a cure for this disease. My company is already developing a promising therapy that has been shown to slow down the progression of this disease." He hesitated, and I knew why. I hated that he was going to make this whole thing contingent up on Miguel doing something for him. It didn't feel right to either of us, but that was what we were faced with.

Miguel looked at Slade. "What kind of therapies? I've searched the world. I know about the gene editing therapy, of course. I would imagine that is what your company is working with."

Slade sat up straighter. "How much would it be worth to you to have a guarantee that Marguerita will have a place in any clinical trial that shows promise? And how much would it be worth to you to have a person that you could call, day or night, and speak with about the advancements being made? To be able to have access, first access, to promising drugs and therapies before the general public?"

"Obviously, all of that would be worth more than all the money in this world to me. What are you saying?"

"Well, as you know, there's a process to getting a drug onto the market. My company often have drugs which are ready to come to market, but they're being reviewed by the FDA and have not yet been released to the public yet. The drugs have gone through all the protocols – the clinical trials, the peer-reviewed studies, the double-blind trials – but they have to go through the review process. In other words, they're really ready to go, but they're held up for months or years. Sometimes they're held up simply because of politics."

Miguel slowly nodded his head. "As you can probably imagine, I would do anything to be able to have access to any of these promising drugs as soon as they are available. To not have to wait for the screening process in your country."

Slade made a temple with his hands. "Mr. Sanchez, here is what I can offer you. I can agree to devote considerable resources towards finding a cure for this disease. $50 million at least. I can hire all the best researchers and pay them top dollar to concentrate on finding a cure. In the meantime, I can assure you that Marguerita will be first in line for any and all clinical trials that come up for promising drugs and therapies. And I can assure you that you can have access to any promising drugs before they hit the open market. All of that might, just might, buy time for Marguerita until a cure can be found."

Miguel appeared to contemplate Slade's words. He stared at Slade, and then stared at me, for what seemed like a long time. I drew a breath and said a little prayer to myself. Finally, he said "what do you want in exchange for this?"

Slade looked at me and then back at Miguel. "I would like you to give your shipment to the Garancinos. And I would like for you to tell Gianni Garancino what Carlotta Garancino has been doing. Tell him about how she has been working to convince you to give your shipment to the Vichellis and tell him why."

Miguel nodded his head. "What kind of reassurances can I get from you that you will be good as your word?"

"You have my word, but, of course, that is not necessarily good enough. I could execute a contract that both of us can sign. The contract will outline all the terms that I just stated. But, I can also understand if you do not want to sign a formal contract with me."

"Yes. It would be very difficult for me to take you to court to reinforce this contract. Of course." He blinked his eyes and then looked at the horizon again, his fingers clasped tightly together. "I enforce my agreements only one way, Mr. Bridgewell. I can only tell you that. In other words, if you do not execute the terms that we agree to, you will be executed instead."

"I understand that completely," I said. "But I would imagine that you would still like the agreement in writing."

In other words, there would be a contract, but a court would not be enforcing it. Miguel's gun would the enforcing agent. I expected that, but it still made me extremely nervous.

He nodded. "Draw it up for me with the terms that you just outlined. Know that if you fail to complete these terms, you will be terminated." Miguel was speaking in crisp terms, all business. It was in complete contrast with how he previously was speaking with us, which was much more emotional. "And I will meet your terms. I do not have any loyalty to Carlotta, although I am a bit sad that my daughter will not get the chance that she was promised."

He did look depressed at that thought, but he was able to shake it off rapidly. I knew why – seeing his wife suffer was tearing him up. He needed to give her hope, and, perhaps more importantly, he needed hope himself.

Slade cleared his throat again. "Mr. Sanchez, I know that I don't have the same degree of clout in the movie industry as does Ms. Garancino. But I do know quite a few people myself. I have many close friends in the business, including movie producers and directors. I also know quite a few agents. As I said, I do not have the quite the same connections as Charlotte, I mean Carlotta, but I can probably offer Mandolina a hand."

Miguel smiled and nodded his head imperceptibly. "You would do that? You do not have to. Simply offering my wife hope is enough. However, I would certainly appreciate it if you could help Mandolina as well. I would be...grateful."

"Of course. I do not know what her acting skills are like, of course, but she is very beautiful. I would be more than happy to bring her to Los Angeles with me. Set her up with an agent, introduce her to some producers and directors and see what might come of it."

Miguel swallowed hard and looked at his hands again. If I wasn't mistaken, I thought I saw tears in his eyes. "Mr.

Bridgewell, you are a good man. A very good man." He smiled. "I always thought you did not kill that man. I can tell in a man's eyes...I can tell their measure."

"I will not let you down." Slade was speaking in formal tones and words, not using contractions, but, rather, was mirroring the speech patterns of Miguel. I knew that was one powerful persuasion technique, and Slade had it down pat.

The two men shook hands. "Bring me the contract today," he said. "And I will not only give my shipment to Mr. Garancino, but I will also tell him what role his daughter Carlotta played in trying to persuade me to give my shipment to the Vichellis. Is there anything else you need for me to do?"

"No," Slade said. "I appreciate all that you have done, and all that you will do. I appreciate it more than you could possibly imagine."

Slade and I stood up, and made a move towards my car. I knew that Slade could have the contract drawn up in a matter of hours – we just needed access to a printer, and there was one on Slade's plane.

However, as we made a move to leave, a black Porsche roared up the drive at top speed. I squinted in the sunlight, trying to see who was behind the tinted glass. I looked over at Miguel, who was shaking his head sadly and speaking in Spanish. Then I looked at Slade, who's face registered shock.

When the car door opened, I soon knew why the two men had such a reaction.

Charlotte Boswell stepped out of the car and glared at the three of us.

This was not going to be pretty.

# Chapter Fifteen

"Hello," Charlotte said directly to Slade. "Somehow I thought that you'd be here. I don't know why I had that hunch, but, here we are, just like I thought."

I looked over at Miguel, who was silently motioning his guards, who had appeared out of nowhere, it seemed. At first, when I saw Charlotte, I thought that perhaps this whole thing was set-up. That Miguel and Charlotte had set up this ambush together. But, that was impossible – Miguel had no clue that we were going to show up at his house today.

Did he?

The guards stood and flanked Miguel, and I got a bit nervous. I tried to tune into everyone's vibrations, but I was stymied. There were too many people that I was trying to read, and nobody was as they seemed. Everyone was suspect, all of a sudden, and it flashed through my brain that I was going to die here.

Slade, however, was cool and unruffled as ever. "Charlotte, don't be so dramatic." He looked over at Miguel, and I knew in his mind that he was hoping, just as I was, that this whole thing wasn't a trap laid out for us. "Mr. Sanchez and I were just parting ways. If you would excuse me, I-"

"You what?" Charlotte said, not letting Slade finish his sentence. She looked from Slade to Miguel and back again. "Miguel, do you mind telling me what is going on here? Why are you speaking with Slade and Serena, when you and I clearly..."

I started to feel a bit relieved, as Charlotte was speaking to Miguel as if she was genuinely asking him why we were there. That would necessarily mean that there wasn't a set-up or a trap.

Didn't it?

"I'm sorry, Senorita, but I have decided to pursue another path. The shipment will go to your father."

Her eyes got wide, and I felt myself let out a breath of relief. My initial reaction was not founded, thank god. It was clear that Miguel was on the level and that Charlotte surprised him as much as she had surprised us.

Regardless, Charlotte showing up was an inconvenience, and that was putting things mildly. Very mildly. Suddenly, things were sped up. They had to be. Slade and I had to get that contract executed and get to Gianni before Charlotte could. I didn't know for sure, but I had the feeling that if Charlotte beat us to the punch, there would be complications in this whole plan.

Charlotte turned to Slade. "Oh, okay. Okay. You think that you out-witted me, didn't you? Didn't you? You thought that you were so clever, finding out about this whole thing. Don't you know that I'll always have Plan B up my sleeve?" She wagged her finger in his face.

Her expression was different as she stood there, pointing at Slade. In all the pictures I ever saw of her in the tabloids, she always had an enormous smile. Her face looked kind, somehow, in those pictures. Soft. I figured that she had practiced in the mirror how her face would look when she was out in the world, which was why the world never knew that she was an absolute psycho. She never looked the part of one, and that was by design.

But, as I watched her, standing there and pointing to Slade, I could see the real Charlotte come out. And she looked like an absolute psycho. Her eyes were so wide that they almost bugged out of her skull. Her mouth was in an absolute grimace and her face was frozen like a Gargoyle. And I could see in those bug eyes of hers the murderous rage that roiled behind them.

She didn't even look like the same person, but I knew that this was her dark soul finally showing in her outward appearance. She looked, for all the world, like somebody who was in the throes of an extreme psychotic break.

I looked over at Miguel, who was motioning for his bodyguards to get closer. And then he motioned them again, and they both drew their weapons. Their guns were pointed at Charlotte, who was unaware of this, as her back was to both of them.

Or was she unaware?

I was soon disabused of this, as she told Slade "I can feel those two goons behind me. Their guns are pointed at me, but I don't care. They can kill me, but as long as I get you first, it'll all be worth it, believe me."

Those words sent chills up my spine.

Then, before I could even think about what was happening, Charlotte brought out a gun and shot Slade. I screamed as Slade crumpled to the ground, right as the bodyguards shot Charlotte in her arm.

She immediately dropped the gun, and she, too, crumpled to the ground.

# Chapter Sixteen

I stood there, in absolute shock, for a few seconds before I went to Slade. I was shaking as I was looking up at Miguel, who was summoning the ambulance. Oh, god, we were in a different country and Slade was going to be treated? I had no idea what kind of hospitals I could expect down here, no idea what kind of care he would get. My mind was racing with what we could do. What could be done.

Fortunately, it looked like Charlotte had missed Slade's vital organs. She was a terrible shot, and, while blood was gushing from his upper chest, he was able to look me in the eye. "I'm going to be fine," he said haltingly. "But don't let them bring me to a hospital here. Get me home."

I nodded my head. Home. Home was way too far away. Texas, on the other hand, was just across the border. "Slade, you need to go to a hospital here to get stabilized, and then I'll call Alex to fly you to a hospital in America. But, for right now, you're going to need a blood transfusion and...something." I was proud of the presence of mind I had as I spoke with him.

I looked over at Charlotte, who was also on the ground, and also seemed to not be in any immediate danger of dying. As much I wanted those bodyguards to just finish her off, it seemed that they were more trained than that. Shoot to alleviate the present situation, not to kill, if killing wasn't necessary. *Just my luck. These are drug dealers with a conscience.*

As if Miguel read my mind, he said "I'm very sorry, Ms. Roberts, I know that you probably would have liked to see Ms. Garancino dead. But we try keep our fatalities to a minimum, especially considering that Ms. Garancino is the daughter of a prominent businessman. You understand, if my guards would have killed her..." He shrugged.

I knew that Miguel had a point. To say that Gianni Garancino wouldn't do business with Miguel would be an understatement. He probably would have killed Miguel, or started a war with him. After all, just because Charlotte hated Gianni, didn't mean that Gianni also hated Charlotte. Chances are that Gianni had no idea how Charlotte felt about him. No clue that she hated him enough to go through all this trouble to undermine him.

A helicopter was soon on the scene. Thank god. An ambulance would take way too long to get here, I thought, and Slade looked like he was hemorrhaging blood at a rapid pace. Two men with a gurney picked up both Slade and Charlotte and put a mask and a blanket over each, and then loaded them up into the chopper.

"Can I come with you?" I asked them, knowing the answer. Of course they weren't going to let me come with them. There was barely room in the chopper for them, let alone another person.

The man spoke in rapid Spanish, and I looked at Miguel helplessly. Miguel, for his part, came over to me and put his hands on my shoulders. "Senorita, they are taking

Mr. Bridgewell and Ms. Garancino to the Hospital Angeles. I know where that is, and I can drive you if you like. They do not have room for you in the helicopter." He smiled. "Of course, you can find it through your GPS on your car, but maybe you'd like some company."

I nodded my head. "I would actually like that, and thank you."

"De nada."

Miguel and I got into my car, and Miguel directed me to the hospital. I could have found it on my GPS, as I had turned it back on after I called Slade to come and help me, but I felt better actually having somebody next to me to guide me.

In the car, Miguel thanked me. "Ms. Roberts," he began, "I know that what I'm about to say is going to sound...different." He struggled to find the right word, I could tell. He was extremely fluent in English, but I did notice that, from time to time, he would have a problem finding certain words. "Different is the right word, I believe. But I hope that you do not believe me to be loco."

I smiled. I knew that loco was Spanish for "crazy." I didn't know may Spanish words, but I knew that one. "I'm sure that I won't find you loco, but go on."

"In my country, God is still very much in our lives. In your country, it is less so. But I have always believed that God would send somebody to me who would help my Marguerita. I have believed that since she was diagnosed. Since she started having her headaches and her muscles started to stiffen. When Mr. Bridgewell told me that he would help her, I knew that God had answered my prayers." He put his hand on mine. "So, do not worry, Ms. Roberts, about Mr. Bridgewell. God will take care of him. Mr.

Bridgewell was sent to help my Marguerita, so God will not let him die."

I looked over at him, and I smiled. "I know. And I don't think that you're loco. I believe that Slade is protected as well." I didn't want to tell him that I knew that Slade would pull through because I, too, had a supernatural belief. My belief came from my innate sixth sense, but I doubted that Miguel, who appeared to be very religious, would understand that.

"You might think it strange," Miguel continued, "that a man like myself, who is in the business that I am in, would have a belief in God." He looked pensive. "I did not believe in God. Not until Marguerita got sick. Then I started to believe. I needed to believe in something, because if I continued to believe in nothing, then there would be no hope."

He looked out the window of the car, and gave me directions to get on the highway and then told me where to turn off. "I am going to retire, Ms. Roberts," he continued from before. "After this shipment to the Garancinos. I have turned my life to Jesus," he said, pronouncing *Jesus* with the Spanish pronunciation, "and I know that He answered my prayers when you and Mr. Bridgewell walked through my doors."

He kissed my hand and directed me to the road that would take me to the hospital.

"I guess that is why you didn't want the contract with the Afghans," I said, stating the obvious.

"Yes, that is true. I have learned what is really important. It is not wealth, it is not power. It is love, Senorita." He took a deep breath. "Love," he said softly.

I smiled as we pulled up to the hospital. "We're here.

And thank you, Mr. Sanchez, for all that you have done for us. Your kindness and generosity will not be forgotten."

"As will yours." Then he smiled. "And please call me Miguel. We are friends now, no?"

I nodded and gave him my hand. "Friends. Please call me Serena."

The two of us went into the hospital and were told to wait in the waiting room until they called us. So, Miguel and I took a seat and waited.

A few hours later, I was able to see Slade. He was recovering in a post-surgical room. The doctors had removed the bullet and gave him a blood transfusion. He was resting comfortably.

He turned his head to me as I sat down next to him and put my hand on his chest. He put his hand on mine. "Serena," he said softly. "I feel like shit."

I smoothed back his dark hair. "Of course you do. You were shot. But you're going to be okay. The doctor said that Charlotte really only nicked you, and didn't damage any arteries or organs or any of that. I guess that you're lucky that she's such a bad shot."

He smiled dreamily. "Yes. Serena, I think that things are going to be fine. Miguel is going to come through for us, and Gianni is going to put Charlotte on ice."

"I think that you're right. By the way, Charlotte is out of surgery as well. Those bodyguards only shot her because she was attacking you. They didn't want to really hurt her."

Slade grimaced. "Too bad. If they would have killed her, our problems would be over." Then he started to laugh. "Oh, imagine if she was out of the way. You and I would have smooth sailing." He gestured with his arm sweeping the air and laughed again.

I smiled. "I think that you're a bit loopy, which is to be expected." I knew something about coming out of surgery, as I had had minor surgeries myself over the years. "Slade, I'm going to have you helicoptered into America as soon as I can have you released from here. Not that this hospital is bad, but I know that you'd rather recover somewhere a bit more...luxurious."

"Why do I care about that? As long as you're by my side, I'll be fine." He took my hand. "And I mean that. You'll always be my side. I hope that you know that."

"I do." I leaned my head down to him and kissed him on the cheek. "Now you get some rest. I'll talk to your doctors and find out when you can be released. Then we'll head back to America."

It was a few days before Slade was stable enough for us to take his plane back to the states, but, as soon as he was, I arranged for it to happen. Miguel agreed to come with us, and even made sure that Charlotte was put into a Mexican jail for shooting Slade. "She will not stay there," Miguel told me, "I only have to make sure that she does not interfere with what I have to do. As soon as everything is arranged with Mr. Garancino, I will make sure that the charges are dropped. I am sure that Mr. Garancino will be more than happy to take care of her on his own."

Everything was arranged then. This isn't to say that I wasn't nervous about what was about to happen. I certainly was. I had no idea how Gianni was going to react to any of this. He was going to find out that his daughter, who was beloved, as far as I could tell, was actually a rat. He might or might not call off the hit on me. He probably would, but I couldn't be sure.

Slade was going to recover at my home in San Diego, with a full-time nurse tending to him until he was completely out of the woods. He was partially out of the woods, of course, but there was always a chance of infection or something like that, so I thought that it was important that there was somebody there to help me.

But first thing was first. We were going to see Gianni and tell him what we needed to tell him. In fact, that was the first thing that we were going to do when we landed. Charlotte might have been neutralized, as she was in jail, but we still found that time was of the essence.

The plan, then, was to go and see Gianni as soon as we arrived back into town. Gianni was anxious to meet with Miguel, of course, because he was waiting to make a deal with Miguel for the large drug shipment that was promised to him. Miguel had called him from his estate in Ciudad to tell him that he was going to agree to work with him on the shipment, not the Vichellis, and they just needed to meet in person to go over the terms. Gianni, of course, was delighted and the two men had arranged over the phone to meet.

What Gianni didn't know, of course, was that Slade and I were also going to be meeting with him. Not that we didn't trust Miguel – we did, of course. But we needed to make sure that the information was conveyed in the right way. Miguel would explain who we were and why were there, and also would explain to Gianni that we needed to be there. If Gianni didn't like it, because this was a sensitive matter that the two men were discussing, then, and only then, would Slade and I step out and let Miguel handle things.

So, we were all on Slade's plane. Slade was resting in one of the beds on the plane, as he still wasn't feeling 100%, while Miguel and I sat and talked. I learned about his life – how he got into drug dealing, his background of extreme poverty, how he met Marguerita and how he felt about Mandolina. He told me some stories of all the times where he almost got into a shootout with other dealers, and how happy he was leaving it all behind.

"Oh, Senorita," he said, putting his hand on mine, "I feel so liberated. I have really enjoyed talking to you. It is like talking with my priest." He smiled slyly. "Yes, I have told my priest all of these stories, too." He looked up at the heavens. "God hears me. The priest has always told me that. And I now believe that is true."

"You too, Miguel," I said. "And believe me, Slade will be working hard, night and day, to find a cure for Huntington's. You'll hopefully have many more happy years with Marguerita."

He looked sad. "I hope that you are right. I told God that I would give up my work, give up what I am doing, if He could send me some hope. Now that you and Slade are here, that is my hope, so I am going to be a man of my word. After this shipment, of course."

"Of course."

I smiled hearing Miguel call Slade by his first name. He was getting more comfortable with both of us. He was becoming a kind of friend, really. And, because I was feeling like he was a friend, I found myself worried about him. What if getting out wasn't as easy as he thought it would be? What if he was going to put himself into danger? What would happen to Marguerita and Mandolina?

"Miguel, I know that you will be, no matter what, but please be careful."

"I will be, Serena. I have already spoken with my second in command, and he is going to make the transition smooth. Do not worry about me, Senorita. I will be fine."

The plane landed, and the three of us got off and into Slade's waiting car. His valet had dropped it off as he usually did whenever Slade traveled on business.

Then we all drove off to see Gianni Garancino.

# Chapter Seventeen

We got Gianni's home, which was, of course, an enormous mansion in Encinitas, a well-to-do seaside town just north of San Diego. The home was set back behind a wide-iron gate, in the middle of a residential neighborhood. It surprised me just a little that he wouldn't be living in a home that was more secluded. It was two story, with arches and colonnades and a Spanish-style roof. There was a reflecting pool right in front of the home, and large palm trees.

We introduced ourselves to the butler, who informed us that Gianni was sitting out by the pool and was expecting Miguel. He looked at Slade and me askance, but said nothing. "Follow me."

The pool area was absolutely gorgeous, with shade trees, waterfalls and a hot tub that would seat at least 8. Gianni was sitting under a large umbrella and table, sipping what looked to be coffee. Tanned and fit, dressed in white shorts, a red t-shirt and sunglasses, with his black curly hair slicked back, he reminded me of an Italian playboy.

He looked at Miguel and then looked at Slade and me, and motioned all of us to sit down. "Miguel," he said, "it's good to see you."

Miguel smiled and nodded, and then introduced us. "Yes, Gianni," he said, which told me that the two men had a friendly relationship. "These are my friends, Mr. Slade Bridgewell and Ms. Serena Roberts."

"I know who you are," he said, looking right at Slade. "You're allegedly dating my daughter." Then he laughed heartily. "And I wish you good luck." Then he shook his head.

Slade looked over at me and shrugged. So far, so good....

"I don't know you, though," he said, looking at me and extending his hand. "But it is a pleasure to meet you all the same."

I shook his hand.

He turned to Miguel. "So, Miguel, we need to talk business here. I need to call Sally, my maid, to come and show these two around the grounds while you and I talk shop." At that, he motioned, and a slight Asian lady came over to us. She was apparently Sally, for she bowed slightly and Gianni asked her to take us to the reserve so that we could see his collection of exotic animals.

Miguel spoke up. "Actually, Gianni, I wanted these two to stay. They're going to be a part of the negotiation."

Gianni's previously friendly expression turned not as friendly. He was wearing sunglasses, so I couldn't see his expression all that well, but his mouth turned down and his face got rigid. I closed my eyes and tuned into his vibrations and I felt that he was angry. Not extremely angry, just frustrated.

"I do not understand," he said to Miguel. "Why wasn't I informed about this?"

"Mr. Garancino," Slade said. "Serena and I need to speak with you about your daughter, Carlotta. There is something that you need to know, and we're the ones to tell you about it. And it all has to do with Miguel and your pending negotiations with him."

Gianni looked mystified by all of this. I figured that he probably had a blind spot where Charlotte was concerned, and I was feeling that I was absolutely right about that assessment. "What do you mean? What does Carlotta have to do with this?"

Slade took a deep breath. "You might not know this, but Carlotta has undermined you at least once. I'm not sure if this is the only time, but I suspect that it's not. Mr. Sanchez, Miguel, can verify this account, but Carlotta was actively working with Miguel against you. She was attempting to persuade Miguel to give his large shipment to your rival family, the Vichellis. She offered to take Miguel's daughter, Mandolina, under her wing and give her a leg-up in Holly-wood if he would give his drug shipment to Vincent Vichelli."

Gianni's cheek twitched furiously when Slade was talking to him. That was the only indication of how angry he was, because we couldn't see his eyes. I wondered if that was part of his MO – meet people out by the pool, so that he had an excuse to wear sunglasses. That way, it would be very difficult to read him. That would help with negotia-tions immensely, I would think.

But, when I tuned into his vibrations, I could feel his anger. It was white-hot, and it seared through me. I had this feeling that Slade was right – Charlotte had done this type of thing more than once. Perhaps she was even caught doing it and Gianni had reprimanded her. Maybe it was on minor things before. This, however, was an important thing, because it would determine which of the rival families would be able to control more assets and turf. In a mafia family, that was everything.

Gianni looked at Miguel. "Is this true?"

"Yes," Miguel said. "It is very true. That is why I wanted them to accompany me. You need to know what kind of a daughter you have. She is very disloyal."

"And," Slade said, feeling emboldened, "I understand that there could be a hit put upon Serena. A hit that was called by Charlotte, I mean Carlotta. A hit that was put into abeyance when I agreed to marry Carlotta."

Gianni bit his lower lip and stared at Serena. He nodded imperceptibly. "Serena Roberts. Forgive me, I did not associate your name with the job that I agreed to do for Carlotta." He chuckled lightly. "I am very sorry, Ms. Roberts. My daughter has always been willful, and, I admit, that she has usually convinced me to do things that I really should not do. But you can be assured, after I have found out what she has done, how disloyal she has been to me, I will no longer do favors for her."

He kissed Serena's hand. "Ms. Roberts, you will not be in danger anymore. You have my assurances for this. As for Carlotta...that's a different story."

I found it interesting that putting a hit on me was considered to be a mere "favor." Never mind, though, if I was safe, than everything was going to work out between Slade and me. I squeezed his hand tightly, and he smiled at me.

"That is the reason why I wanted Mr. Bridgewell and Ms. Roberts here with us," Miguel said. "I needed you to know what your daughter did, and I wanted you to cancel the hit on Ms. Roberts. She is a good woman." He hesitated. "And I also wanted to tell you that I plan on retiring.

If you would like a long-term contract, than I can do that. It just will not be me who will be your supplier. It will be my second-in-command, whose name is Guillermo. Guillermo Gonzales. He will be taking over all my long-term contracts."

Gianni nodded and patted Miguel on the back. "I understand. This is a rough life. I don't blame you for getting out. I've thought the same thing many times, believe me. I've always thought that retirement is just around the corner." Then he shook his head. "But I think that I'm addicted to this life. I will probably die before I retired, I'm afraid."

Miguel looked over at the two of us. "Why don't you find Sally and she can show you the exotic animals? Gianni and I have to go over the terms of our contract, and I do not want to bore you with the details."

At that, Sally appeared again and smiled. We followed her to a motorized golf cart and she drove us through the woods. We came upon an area where there were Wallabies, Chimpanzees, Monkeys and Macaws. The Chimps were a family, apparently, with two older Chimps and several babies. The Monkeys were tiny and lived in the trees. The Wallabies hopped around freely, many with babies in their pouches. I was amused by the antics of these animals, and I could feel their vibrations. They seemed perfectly content, and why shouldn't they? They were in a tropical paradise, with plenty of trees, grass and room to run.

"Who cares for these animals?" I asked Sally.

"Mr. Garancino has a special zoo-keeper who lives on-site," she said, pointing to a house that was in the woods. "He lives over there."

I nodded, feeling enchanted by the animals running around. I was expecting to see Llamas, which was the usual exotic animal that was kept by eccentric people, but this was an entire menagerie. In addition to the bigger animals, there were smaller exotic foxes and other types of animals that I didn't necessarily recognize.

Slade and I walked through the forest, laughing at the animals, and looking at each other from time to time. This was probably the best feeling of my life – just being able to be there, out in the open, and, hopefully, Slade and I would be together for the rest of our lives.

---

After about an hour, we got back in the golf cart, and Sally drove us back to the pool area. She drove over rocks and through the trees until we got to where the two men were still sitting, now sipping a glass of wine. I would imagine that the negotiations had ended, because they seemed to be chatting casually. Their body language told me that they were not hashing out tense terms, but were talking like friends.

Gianni stood up when he saw the two of us. "Hello," he said, "Miguel and I were just talking about you two. I would like to apologize again for my daughter." He shook his head and spoke in Italian. "You think that you know what they are doing, but, you never really do, do you?" He then put his hand on my shoulders. "Now, Ms. Roberts, I do not want you to fear for your life. There is nothing that Carlotta can do now to convince me to harm you in any way. I have already talked to my men, and I have given all of them a stand-down order."

I felt such a sense of relief, as I knew that Gianni was sincere. I wondered what he was going to do to Charlotte once he saw her again. I didn't really care, though. I was curious more than anything.

"Thank you, Mr. Garancino," I said. I squeezed Slade's hand, and he smiled at me.

"I would like to invite you to stay for dinner," he said, pointing to a long table by the pool. "I have an enormous spread, and I hope that I can provide anything that you would like. I do like to make that my guests are happy."

"We'd like that," Slade said, looking at me. "If you have vegan options."

Gianni smiled and chuckled. "Vegan options, gluten-free options, you name it. Living out here in Southern California, you have to be prepared for anything. So, let us go over and toast to one another and enjoy the sunshine and the beautiful food."

That night, we talked, laughed, drank wine and ate great food. Gianni was charming, Miguel was a great conversationalist, and Slade and I couldn't be closer. The evening was beautiful, albeit cool, but Gianni turned on some heat lamps as the night wore on.

Slade and I were finally in a good place. I hoped and prayed that we would stay there.

# Chapter Eighteen

## Serena - Six Months Later

Luke was down to visit, and so were Mark, Amy, and Christopher. My father and Caroline were as well. They were all here in San Diego to finally see Slade and I join together for eternity. I never thought that it would happen. There were some really, really dark days. But, after that magical evening with Gianni and Miguel, everything started to fall into place.

It started with the imprisonment of Charlotte. Turned out the murder of Rachel, Santino's teacher, was covered up by Gianni. Murder doesn't have a statute of limitations, of course, and, when Gianni found out that Charlotte was a rat, he set about to make her pay.

And pay she did. She could never be tried again for the other murder, because she was tried and convicted for that one. Granted, she only served a short time in a juvenile detention for that other murder, but the law was the law, and trying her again for that one would be double jeopardy.

Ah, but the murder of Rachel...that was a different thing. Gianni called off the dogs that were protecting her, and, suddenly, there were numerous witnesses who were found and ready to roll all over Charlotte. The prosecutor got the ball rolling, and, before anybody knew what had happened, Charlotte was arrested.

The publicity that surrounded her arrest was unlike anything I had ever seen. Ever. It surpassed the publicity for Slade's trial by a magnitude of 10. Charlotte was on top of the Hollywood heap, ready to conquer the movie world. She even was nominated for an Oscar, and won, even though she couldn't attend the ceremony because she was in prison at the time.

So, yeah, she was an Oscar winner and was going to prison, maybe for life. And the tabloids and 24-hour news channels had an absolute field day. Her life was trashed, day and night, night and day, all over every channel and Social Network you could think of. Every time I logged onto the computer, her face would come up. There was story after story after story about her, because, suddenly, everyone wanted to tell what they knew.

And she was still awaiting trial. Everybody knew that she was guilty, and, now that she was no longer protected by one of the wealthiest and most powerful mafia network in Southern California, nobody was afraid to say what they knew anymore. It was a feeding frenzy unlike anybody had ever seen. And, considering that Southern California also had the privilege of being the epicenter of the OJ trial, to say that the Charlotte feeding frenzy was unlike anything anybody had ever seen was saying a lot. There were no nightly "dancing Itos," but that was coming, I was sure about that.

The upshot was that everyone now knew that Charlotte

was absolutely psychotic. Everyone knew all the drugs that she did, how many people she screwed, and how many people she screwed over. Men who dated her came out to the press and told all. Women she dated did the same. On and on and on, until even I finally got tired of reading it. It was all *schadenfreude* for awhile, because, after all, she destroyed an innocent life in Slade and attempted to destroy my life as well. She deserved all the trashing that she got. And if she went to prison for life, oh well.

But, there came a time when I finally got over my hatred for her and just felt pity. How awful it must be to have to live with such seething resentment and deep insecurity, so much that you want to ruin everything that you touch. I wouldn't wish her mental state on anybody, and, well, I started to feel compassion for her.

Slade, on the other hand, did not feel compassion for her at all. He wanted her to rot, and I really didn't blame him.

But, that was all really besides the point. After the whole Charlotte threat went to the wayside, Slade and I made up for lost time. And we got engaged.

He popped the question to me when we took a trip to Northern California to see the redwood trees. Looking at these trees, which have been around since pre-historic times, I knew how small and insignificant I really was. To think that, long, long after I passed into the earth, these trees would still be around, was breath-taking. The redwoods can live up to 2,000 years. I wished that they could talk.

In the middle of the redwood forest, Slade got down on one knee and presented me the most beautiful ring I had ever seen. It was a canary yellow diamond, princess-cut and perfect. I said yes, of course. As if there was any other answer.

Now, today, was my big day. I wasn't going to have a major shin-dig like Dalilah. After all, this was my second marriage, so I really didn't want to make a fuss. I wasn't much for fusses anyhow. It was pretty much going to be me and Slade on a private beach, about 50 of mine and Slade's closest friends and family in attendance.

The close friends and family included Miguel, and a getting-better-every-day Marguerita. Mandolina would also be in attendance. Slade and Mandolina had become close, as Slade made good on his promise to introduce her to the power players he knew, and the producers who saw Mandolina were impressed. She was already getting a few movie parts – mainly as an extra on horror movies - but some of our greatest actors started their careers in that same way.

But Marguerita was the real marvel. True to his word, Slade got her into some major clinical trials, and they were really helping her. He also devoted millions and as many bright minds as he could hire to find a cure for the disease. He was coming up with breakthrough after breakthrough, which he would excitedly tell me every evening. Finding a cure for Huntington's had become his passion, and it was wonderful to see.

---

I walked to Slade, my feet bare, wearing a simple white dress with no veil. I just let my hair flow. Slade was standing at the end of the beach, wearing a white tux with no shoes. He had never looked more handsome. As I took his hands, and looked into his eyes, I knew. I knew that when I said "til death do us part," that I meant it. We would truly be together until one of us died. When he looked at me, I knew that he knew it too.

I sighed as we said our vows and the minister told Slade to kiss the bride. He kissed me, long and passionate, and everyone cheered and threw rose petals as we made our way on the carpet towards the other end of the beach.

Afterwards, everyone gathered in one large tent and good food and great alcohol flowed. Pictures were taken, everyone had a great time, and the live band was excellent. This was the most magical night of my life, and I never thought that anything could be better.

Of course, Bella and Gigi were also in attendance. They ran around the beach, their tiny little bodies running around and around until they were exhausted. Now, in the tent, they went around to the different tables and begged for scraps. Everyone loved the little dogs, and I posed for more than one picture with them in my arms, with Slade wrapped around me from behind.

"I love you, Slade," I said to him. "And I always will."

"I love you Serena," he said, "And I always will."

And, with those few words, I knew that my life was complete.

# Chapter Nineteen

## Serena - Ten Years Later

It was time. Slade was going to Oslo, Norway, to pick up his Nobel Prize. He had finally isolated the right gene to edit, and had finally, after years and years of 20 hour days, and countless false starts and frustrations, found the cure for Huntington's Disease. Suddenly, getting a diagnosis for Huntington's was no longer a death sentence, but was curable. Nobody thought that it could happen in a lifetime, but Slade showed what persistence and genius could do.

In the process, Marguerita was cured, and Miguel had become a life-long friend. His daughter, Mandolina, had also become a major player in Hollywood. Her small roles in horror movies got the attention of some independent directors, who cast her in supporting roles in various movies. Then came her big break in a romantic comedy that was the sleeper of the year, much the way that *Pretty Woman* was – something that nobody saw coming, and revitalized the genre. And she suddenly became A-List.

Slade was responsible, at least in part, for both of these triumphs, and Miguel could not be more grateful. True to his word, he had long since quit the drug-dealing business, and was living a relatively quiet life on his sprawling ranch. He had actually opened a restaurant in Ciudad, and it was thriving. But he didn't spend much time there, after he got it up and running – most of his time was spent with Marguerita, for he knew how valuable time with her really was. True, she wasn't dying anymore, thanks to Slade, but nonetheless, Miguel knew how important she was. He showed her every day how much she meant to him.

As for Slade and me – we had three children. The twins came about a year after we were married, and I named them Olive and Margot. Olive was named for my mother Olivia, and, since Luke already had a little girl named Olivia, I decided that Olive was a better name. And Margot, of course, was named for Slade's late mother.

The third child, a boy named Luka, named after Luke, of course, came two years later. All the kids were a handful, but I somehow managed them. I kept my law career, as a partner, of course, but I tried to work as few hours as possible so that I could spent as much time with the kids as I could.

Life was as perfect as I could have ever imagined.

And I could imagine a lot.

# Fearless: Chapter One

## Dalilah

"Sorry I'm late," I said to Kyle, who was tapping his toes and crossing his arms as I rushed into the tiny changing room.

"Doll," he said, "you've been late a lot lately. What's going on?"

I swallowed hard, knowing that I really couldn't tell him the truth. Which was that I drank a few too many shots and ended up in the apartment of some guy in Queens. Considering that this art studio was located in SoHo, which was a considerable subway ride away from Queens, it was no wonder that I was a half hour late.

"Sorry," I said. "It won't happen again."

"Better not. You better be glad that you got that beautiful boy Seth taking care of your pretty little ass. Otherwise, you might be out on the street. Because one more tardy, and you're gone."

I bit my lip, knowing that he was absolutely right. I had

long since declared absolute financial independence from my parents, over their objections, and this part-time job modeling nude for art students was really my only source of income. Well, that, and my side gigs modeling for established artists in the Village. Between all of these gigs I made enough, just barely, to afford my studio apartment in SoHo.

Seth was much more established than myself. He was 21 and graduated early from Harvard and had taken his first job in the financial district. So he was making bank. Which he constantly threw in my face. Still, he more or less took care of me and made sure that I had groceries in the house. And the sex with him was pretty good, I guess. The high school rumors that were circulating about his Johnson did prove to be pleasantly true, which was a plus.

Kyle was still crossing his arms as I hurriedly changed out of my clothes and into my white robe. I hated to keep the class waiting, I really did. Quite frankly, I was embarrassed to be in that situation. But it did seem to be happening more and more frequently for whatever reason.

Seth knew about my extracurricular activities and seemed unconcerned about it all. "You do what you want, Dalilah," he had said. "As long as you keep doing that thing you do with your tongue, I'm good to go."

Permission having been granted, I had the freedom to do whatever it was that I wanted, within my budget, of course. And I took it. I was 20. If I had gone to college, I would be going to keggers and screwing random strangers, because that's what you do in college. That's what Alaina was doing over at NYU. So, I felt that I was somehow fulfilling what might have been expected of me had I gone the traditional route of college.

Which I didn't. My parents let me leave the house at 16 to go and live with Uncle Nick and Aunt Scotty in

Connecticut, because I had expressed a desire to get back into art in general and the art scene in New York City in particular. I think that my parents really wanted me to go to college, but they weren't the type to demand anything from me, preferring that I learn to make my own way in life.

"That's what you have always done, Dalilah," mom had said. "Always. So, far be it for me to stop you now. We want you to make your own decisions about your life, because you need to own what you do. Nobody else can own your life but you. Remember that."

That had made a lot of sense to me. They were basically saying that I needed to find my own path without their pushing me into anything. Alaina was jealous of this, of course. Her parents were forcing her to apply to every Ivy League college there was, which she did, being the ever dutiful daughter. Of course, she was really like a female Eddie Haskell, in that she was obsequious to a fault to the face of her elders, but, behind their backs, she was the wildest girl I had yet to know. And she was over 1200 miles away from her suffocating parents, who still lived in the Kansas City area, so she was pretty much into everything. Prescription drugs, alcohol, even some street stuff that I would never think about trying. I heard too many horror stories from my father to ever think about doing some of the things that Alaina was doing.

But alcohol? Oh, yeah. I was sucking that stuff down like water. Because I was still directionless. No matter how much I tried, I couldn't seem to get the muse back. So, I modeled for art classes, hoping against hope that these young students would inspire some kind of spark of creativity in me again. But they never did.

So, I pretty much did the nude modeling gigs to pay the bills and nothing more. The university gigs paid pretty low by New York City standards – only around $25 an hour. But the private gigs that I managed to score paid around $100 an hour, so I was able to maintain my financial independence from my parents, however tenuously, while I pretty much waited for my well-spring of creativity to activate in me once more.

In the meantime, I had my bottles of Cuervo and Jack, my random men, and Seth whenever I wanted him. These things kept me company. So did Alaina, who was not only experimenting with drugs but with her sexuality as well. She kissed me one drunken night at my apartment, and we ended up in bed together. It had happened three times since then, and it was…nice. I guess. About as good as Seth, really.

I changed into my robe and glared at Kyle. "What?"

"Missy, if you weren't so goddamned physically flawless, I would have canned your sweet ass a long time ago. Now get out there."

I rolled my eyes, and stepped out in front of the waiting class. They were buzzing restlessly. I saw quite a few canvasses with no students behind them, as the students in question obviously had gotten fed up and left. There was a guy sitting on the back table, tossing a ball in the air, while a girl sat at his feet, playing with her phone and grabbing onto his leg playfully. A few students were drawing and painting diligently, but, mainly, the students were in various stages of boredom and ennui.

I took off my robe and stood in front of the class. Immediately, the buzzing stopped, and the students' eyes were trained on me. I sighed a little bit in relief, and laid down on the blanket that was placed on the hard surface. Within two minutes, every student was behind their canvas, painting diligently.

I wanted to address the class and apologize for my lateness. It wasn't like me to be so disrespectful, but I had really drank to the point of blacking out the previous night, so getting up and making this 9 AM class was more than a challenge. Especially since I had to come from Queens. How I made it to Queens last night in my inebriated state was a mystery that I had not yet contemplated. I could only assume that Mystery Boy had called a cab for both of us to take from the Village bar that I was getting hammered in.

*God, I hope there were condoms involved.* I had no desire to end up back in the clinic to get another prescription for antibiotics or whatever it is that they give you when you end up with chlamydia. Yeah, virtually everyone I knew had that particular disease at least once, but it didn't make it any less embarrassing. And, god forbid I get something else that wasn't so curable. I had thus far been lucky that way, unlike Janelle, who hung out with Alaina and me. She was exposed to the herp, the gift that keeps on giving, and was constantly dealing with painful outbreaks that caused her to have to often miss class.

As I laid there, the students dispassionately staring at me, and then quickly tending to their canvases, I started to feel the familiar feeling of wanting to hurl. I really think that I was still drunk when I started this particular gig, and the alcohol had finally worked its way through my system, and all that I wanted right at that moment was some kind of bucket or something. I swallowed hard, and stared at the lights, hoping that they might distract me. I imagined that, since Kyle was already so pissed at me for being late, he probably would end up canning me if I would have puked all over the floor. And getting up and running to the bathroom was not an option. These students were in the flow, and my leaving right at that moment would have been more than unfair to them.

*Damn, this is the longest half hour of my life.* Thank god I was a half hour late, because I literally didn't think that I ever could have laid there for the full hour. I imagined that the students might have painted my face a bit green, then laughed to myself for thinking that.

Finally, the class was over, and the students started packing up their tools and canvases. They lingered around the classroom, talking to one another, trying hard not to look at me as I stood up and put on my white robe and slippers. I quickly ran back to the back room, as the urge to vomit once again presented itself, and I finally found relief in hovering over the toilet.

Kyle came over disapprovingly. "Not preggers, I hope. Aw, but, then again, that might be interesting. Give the kids a different kind of female form to draw."

I looked up at him. "No, not pregnant. I'm using something. Just a long night last night, that's all."

"How long?" he asked, his hands on his hips. Kyle could be such a queen sometimes.

"I left the strange Queens apartment at 8 this morning. Hence my being a half hour late. You know how long it takes to get here from Queens with all the transfers."

Kyle just shook his head. "Do your parents have any idea what you're doing? Aren't you supposed to, you know, be an art student instead of an art model?"

"No offense, Kyle, and I hope that this doesn't sound too arrogant. But I studied all the masters, starting when I was five years old. Between the age of 5 and 11, I was more prolific than almost any working artist you could name today. I had showings at the *Luhring* and the *Bonakdar*," I said, referencing two Chelsea galleries that worked with artistic powerhouses from around the globe. "So I really don't know what I could possibly learn in a classroom that hasn't already been self-taught."

Kyle narrowed his eyes. "You do know that I can Google what you just said, don't you, Dalilah Gallagher?"

I shrugged my shoulders. "Go right ahead. I'm not lying about that."

He looked skeptical and brought out his phone. After a minute or so, his eyes got wide in astonishment. "You really weren't kidding. My god, your work was so…"

"Mesmerizing and raw?" I said. "Heard it all before."

"You were how old when you got these showings?" he asked, as he flipped through the Google images of my work.

"I was 10 when I got my first major showing. I also got a showing at the *Magda Danysz* in Paris that same year."

"10. For the love of god, what have you been doing lately?"

I shrugged my shoulders. "I quit. I lost my voice and my inspiration. I found that I no longer had anything to say."

"Nothing to say? You mean to tell me that you were a has-been by the age of 11?"

"That's exactly what I'm telling you. But, art has always been the only thing that interests me, so I'm desperately trying to get it back. To find my voice again. It hasn't been easy. I thought that just being in the environment with fledgling artists, and especially being in the environment of the established ones for which I model, would inspire me to pick up my brush again. But I have found that I still go home and stare at an empty canvas night after night."

"Oh, I see. So, you go out to the bars and get shit-faced so that you don't have to sit home and stare at that canvas."

I put my finger on my nose and smiled. "You catch on quickly."

He shook his head. "Dalilah. Running from your problems isn't going to solve them."

"No, but getting shit-faced helps me forget about them for a least a short period of time. They're still there, as big as life, when I'm living in reality. But, for a few hours, as I sip my Tanqueray and tonic, my inadequacies seem less so. It's merciful, really."

"You know, you mentioned once that you left school at age 16 and moved here. Maybe that has something to do with it, too. Why you're wondering through life with all the direction of a feather in the wind."

"I'm sure that didn't help," I said, honestly. "But school wasn't doing me any good, either. It's very hard to concentrate in class when you're studying something that you've already mastered before the age of 7. Which would encompass most of the material in my high school courses. Even the advanced courses. I was about ready to jam my pencil into my brain, I was so bored."

"So," he said. "You've been in this city for three years then. And in that time, you've accomplished…."

"Let's not go into that, okay? I'd rather not have to contemplate it."

"You've answered my question," he said.

"I'm glad," I said. "Now, if you don't mind, I'm going to get dressed and get on the subway and go…somewhere." I didn't really know where I was going to go. Seth was working, of course, and Alaina was in class. Unfortunately, today was one of the days that I didn't have a private gig. On such days, I found myself wandering the city endlessly. More often than not, I got into trouble.

"Well, okay, then. But, little girl, tomorrow morning. 9 sharp. One more late day, and you'll find yourself on the street. Are we clear?"

"Crystal," I said.

I got dressed and went down to the street. I went up to a street vendor and grabbed a bagel and lox and sat down on a bench to eat it.

On the other bench was an extraordinarily handsome and well-dressed man. Despite the fact that it was 50 degrees, which meant that I was dressed in a cardigan, the man had on a trench coat. His black hair was slicked back, and his eyes were a cerulean blue. In spite of myself, I found myself staring at him. He looked so familiar....

I shook my head, and continued to eat my bagel. But I soon became aware that he was trying to catch my eye. I could see it in my peripheral vision. So, I looked up again.

Then it struck me. I had seen him before. Many times before, in fact. It never occurred to me that this guy seemed to be everywhere I went, for whatever reason. It just registered when I took a good look at his face.

I smiled, for he was staring at me. His stare was penetrating and cold, and it made me feel uncomfortable. He raised his cup of coffee to his lips and continued to stare.

Finally, he held out his hand for me to shake. "Blake," he said. "Blake Nottingham."

"Dalilah," I said, although I had the feeling that he already knew my name. Just a hunch, but I was rarely wrong about such things. "Dalilah Gallagher."

"Dalilah. So, what brings you to this bench in the middle of the day?"

I shrugged. "Don't really have a place to go, I guess. Except home. But that's just too depressing. What about you?"

He smiled a little. "I'm the boss. I set my own hours." It was then that he gave me one of his cards. *Blake Nottingham, CEO, Nottingham Industries*, the card read. I recognized the name of the company, for it was a large software developer, with its world headquarters in Lower Manhattan.

*Eh, so he's a big wig. So what? So is my dad.* But there was something in those eyes of his that were very much not like my father's. My dad's eyes were kind, humorous. Full of life and warmth. He never took himself all that seriously, and he had some serious passion for my mother, even after all these years. They kind of grossed me out when I lived there, because I knew that, unlike most of my friend's parents, mine did It. A lot.

But this guy....he looked demanding. Cruel, even.

I shifted uncomfortably in my bench, and brought my bagel to my lips again. I looked over, and he was still staring at me. Lustfully. That was the only way that I could have explained it. He looked like he wanted my lips to be some-place else, other than on that bagel.

Finally, I finished my bagel and looked over my shoulder and saw a bus approaching. "Well, it's really good to meet you, Blake," I said, gesturing to the bus. "But I have to go."

"But you said that you didn't have anywhere to go," Blake said, his eyes now registering hurt. "I was hoping to get to know you better."

*Stalker.* "Well," I said. "Sorry to disappoint. I'll uh, see you later." And the funny thing was, I knew that I was right about that.

Somehow I was going to run into him again. He wanted something from me, that was clear.

And I had a pretty good feeling on what that was.

**Grab your copy...**
**vinci-books.com/fearless**

## About the Author

Annie currently lives in San Diego with her two fur-babies, Bella and Toby, and her significant other, Joey. When she's not writing, she's busy reading, cycling all over town, watching cooking shows or classic old movies on TCM (Cary Grant is her favorite) and occasionally watching trashy television shows.